WRONG BED,
Right Guy

A COME UNDONE NOVEL

Praise for Wrong Bed, Right Guy

WRONG BED, *Right Guy*

A COME UNDONE NOVEL

KATEE ROBERT

Entangled Publishing, LLC
2614 South Timberline Road
Suite 109
Fort Collins, CO 80525
Visit our website at www.entangledpublishing.com.

Brazen is an imprint of Entangled Publishing, LLC. For more information on our titles, visit www.brazenbooks.com.

Edited by Heather Howland
Cover design by Heather Howland

ISBN   978-1-62061-292-7

Manufactured in the United States of America

First Edition July 2012

To Tom

CHAPTER ONE

Tonight she was seducing her Mr. Right.

As soon as she found the courage to take the first step, that is.

The staircase before her seemed to stretch up forever. Elle knew better—there were only thirteen steps leading to the loft above the gallery, the same as always. It didn't feel like the same, though. Were the walls narrower than before? She adjusted her coat, trying to get some air circulating. She would have preferred to go without since it was too warm out for coats, even this late at night, but it wasn't like she could waltz upstairs wearing only lingerie, could she?

Elle gripped the banister until her knuckles went white. Was she really going to do this? It wasn't too late to turn back, to pretend she'd never had this insane idea in the first place. Things would go on just like they'd always been, with her working at the gallery and Nathan being completely unaware she was interested in him.

The thought settled like lead in her stomach. No. If she backed out now, she'd never get things moving between them. Nathan sure as heck hadn't caught any of her blatant hints. If she was going to stave off her mother's matchmaking efforts and land a guy she could stomach being around, it was time for a more direct approach.

Last year, when Ian recommended applying for the art coordinator job at the gallery, she'd balked—could she really work under one of her brother's military buddies? But she'd walked into the gallery and was instantly swept away. Though Nathan focused more on scrap-metal sculpting, the galleries he owned displayed every type of art. It was as if someone pulled the idea of what heaven would look like straight from her head.

Then there was Nathan himself. She'd expected someone like Ian—intense, protective, and sporting some serious anger issues. Nathan wasn't like that at all. He was quiet and, though his sense of humor was almost wicked, he was never less than polite. It didn't hurt that he was beautiful, either—tall with golden blond hair and blue eyes that always seemed to twinkle. Most days, they spent hours talking about art and arguing theory, which made him the full package. Exactly the kind of refined man her mother had been pushing her to find, though he was a far sight better than any of the ones she'd forced Elle into dinner with.

She hesitated, her weight balanced between two steps. Okay, so they didn't have the kind of chemistry that sizzled when they were in the same room together, and he wasn't the kind of guy she'd have chosen for herself—but that was exactly the problem. She'd already learned the hard way that she had bad taste in men, and an overwhelming level of attraction brought nothing but heartache. Just because Nathan didn't rock her socks off on a non-academic level didn't mean it couldn't work up to more. And tonight would go a long way toward fixing that.

She hoped.

It took every ounce of willpower to keep moving up the stairs. By the time she reached the top, her breath came in short pants as if she'd just run a mile. Pathetic. She could do better. Really, she could.

Straightening, Elle forced herself to walk down the narrow hallway toward the single door at the end. Judging from his car in the parking lot, Nathan would be sleeping in the loft above the gallery this weekend. She'd guessed as much when he mentioned he'd started planning a new piece today. When he started a new project, he was like a man possessed, focused solely on bringing it to life.

The door loomed, dark wood that contrasted with the pale green of the walls. Normally she found the coloring soothing, but there was no battling the anxiety pulsing through her. The knob was startlingly cold against her palm as she stepped into the shadows of the loft. In the single lamp's light, she took in the oversized canvas sitting in the living room that Nathan used to map out his sculptures before he started welding. It was still in the early stages so she wasn't sure where he was going with it yet, but the violent reds and blacks raised the small hairs on the back of her neck. Elle wouldn't like this one, she was sure of it. Still, it would end up being sold for a truly outstanding price—all Nathan's work did.

Elle bypassed the spare bedroom and skirted the kitchen counter, heading to the master bedroom. Her heartbeat picked up until she was sure it would burst from her chest. Still not too late to back out…

She unbuttoned the coat and carefully laid

it over the barstool. Goose bumps rose over her bare skin as the chilled air wrapped around her body. Elle smoothed down the ruffles on the bottom of her lingerie and tried to focus. The short slip didn't cling like the other stuff she'd tried on, and though it was thin, the ruffles over her chest and hips hid the essentials from view. She ran a hand over the silky fabric covering her stomach. The simplicity of the middle had struck her as a great contrast to the ruffles. It was feminine without shoving her outside her comfort zone.

She rolled her eyes. What a joke—she was so outside her comfort zone right now, she didn't even know where the line was anymore. Buying lingerie had seemed like a really good idea at the time, but standing here in the dark, she suddenly wasn't so sure.

Biting her lip, she grabbed a condom out of her coat pocket, wondering where the heck she was going to put it. Maybe she should just leave it… No. While she wanted a family eventually, getting pregnant tonight would be a freaking nightmare. She'd only been on the Pill a month. What if it wasn't working yet? She searched her body for an appropriate hiding place and came up empty. Seriously, what was she supposed to do with the condom? Hold it in her hand? Stick it into the top of the lingerie? She so wasn't cut out for this sort of thing.

Clutching the condom like a life preserver, Elle took a deep breath and opened the door just enough to slip through. She'd only been in this room a handful of times before, all on some errand for Nathan, but even in the pitch-black darkness, she knew the gigantic bed was directly across from the door. Okay. She could do this. She was woman, hear her roar.

Too bad Elle felt more like a kitten than a lioness.

• • •

Gabe was having the most fantastic dream.

A woman climbed into his bed and touched his shoulder, a breathy whisper slipping past her lips. He rolled over and stretched, intrigued by that little whisper, wondering what his subconscious had in store for him tonight. She shifted close enough that he could just barely feel her warmth seep through the sheet covering his hips. *Mmm, this was going to be good.*

Needing more from her, he draped an arm around her waist and pulled her body against his side. She was a slight, tender little thing, completely opposite of what he usually went for. Guess his subconscious decided it was time for a change. When she ran a timid hand from his shoulder to his hip and pressed herself against him, he decided maybe different was better, because this felt too damn good to be real.

Who knew crashing at his little brother's gallery was the way to dreaming up a fantasy woman? All Gabe had cared about after he got off the plane from Los Angeles was finding a meal and a beer, so he'd jumped at the chance when Nathan called to welcome him home. Obviously it was the best idea he'd ever had.

Gabe sighed and settled in for the rest of what he hoped would be a fabulous night of sleep—exactly what he needed after the chaos he'd dealt with in Los Angeles—but then her lips found his neck and she shivered against him.

Wait a damned second. Those lips weren't fantasy. They were *real*. *Real* lips and a decidedly *real* shiver.

Gabe's eyes flew open and searched the shadows beside him. Holy shit, he wasn't dreaming at all. There was a woman in his bed.

Oblivious to his rude awakening, she kissed his jaw, so soft and sweet it took his breath away.

Staying in bed *so* wasn't the right thing to do, but an ache started in his chest—a craving so strong he couldn't ignore it. Lifting his chin to give her better access, he wondered what he should do. Toss her out on her ass? Let her rub that soft body all over him? Wait, that was wrong. Skeezy. He didn't even know who this chick was.

A few years ago, not knowing the girl in his bed wouldn't have stopped him, but that wasn't his life anymore. He didn't want to be that guy.

She kissed him again, this time perilously close to his lips. Gabe couldn't think with her mouth on him, so he put his hands on her shoulders and angled away to create some distance. The woman turned her head and pressed an openmouthed kiss to his knuckles, temporarily shorting out his brain. Oh, God. Gabe should get out of bed and demand to know what the hell was going on. How many times had he tried to stem the tide of loneliness with a one-night stand, only to wake up the next morning, more empty than he'd been before?

But before he could disentangle their bodies, she ran her hand down his chest, her fingertips dancing along the edge of the suddenly not-thick-enough sheet. Gabe bit back a groan. To hell with it. He couldn't forget her name the morning after if he didn't know what it was to begin with, right? She could chase away the bitter cold inside him for a little while. He'd deal with the consequences tomorrow.

"Are you sure?" Christ, his voice was so roughed up from sleep that it barely sounded like his own.

Her little sigh seemed to roll through his entire body. Gabe found himself holding his breath as he waited for her answer. When she spoke, it was so soft he almost missed the words. "I'm sure."

Working in his nightclubs, he spent a lot of time around bartenders and brassy dames—chicks who knew what they wanted and didn't hesitate to go after it. He liked how different this woman was, how she trembled against him when her arms wound around his neck, how her tongue darted out, so damn tentative, and traced his bottom lip. He opened to her and his first taste, all peppermint and woman, made his head spin. It felt…clean. Innocent. Perfect.

He wasn't exactly a magnet for innocent girls—not with the tats covering so much of his upper body and crawling up his neck. They took one look at him and decided he wasn't the knight in shining armor type.

They were right.

But maybe he wanted to be.

Gabe shut off that nagging part of his brain and let himself enjoy this new experience. Her hand trailed up his chest, pausing over his pecs before finally cupping his jaw. Each touch was light and almost...*treasuring*. It burned through Gabe and his body instantly jumped to attention, demanding he do more than hold this woman. But instead of yanking her on top of him like he wanted to, he touched the back of her neck, relishing the softness of her skin, marveling at how fragile she felt, and ran his other hand down her side. Ruffles and satin and...more ruffles. What in God's name was this chick wearing?

Finally, he found the silky skin of her thigh. Gabe went still as she shivered, making a noise in the back of her throat. That little whimper, more than anything else, undid him. He had to have her. *Now*.

Deepening the kiss, he hooked his hand around the back of her thigh and lifted her easily, settling her over his hips, a leg on either side of him. She gave a little yelp that turned to a moan when he rocked against her, only two thin pieces of cloth between them. Letting go of her neck, he moved just enough to kick down the sheet—one problem down, one to go.

She gasped, pulling away long enough to say, "You're *naked*."

Wasn't that the point? Before Gabe could ask, she was kissing him again, bolder this time. He pulled off her dress thing, nearly cursing when she had to let go of him to toss it aside. But then she was back, keeping up the torturously light stroking. He leaned up and took one of her nipples in his mouth, sucking hard until her hips jerked. Every one of her responses was so...he didn't even know. It was as if she'd never been touched before.

Gabe took her other nipple, lashing it with his tongue until her entire body quivered. He ran his hand down her stomach, cupping her through her silk panties. Even with so little foreplay, she was ready for him. He traced the edge of the fabric, hooking it with his fingers, barely touching her heated skin. She cried out and he gave up teasing to push one finger inside her.

Feeling her wet warmth clamp around him, the desire to flip her over and bury himself in her nearly made Gabe pass out. No. He needed to slow down. Savor her while he could. Working her with his finger, he moved back to her first breast, covering it with open mouthed kisses as he pushed a second finger into her. Gabe twisted his wrist, searching for the spot that would drive her wild.

Her entire body shuddered when he found what he was looking for, mercilessly stroking it with his fingertips. "Oh…oh God…it feels so… I've never…"

Never? Christ. This was the best night ever. Gabe wrapped his free arm around her waist, holding her in place as he kept it up until she arched, throwing her head back, her nails digging into his shoulders as she cried out.

He'd never heard anything so beautiful in his entire life.

Now. Gabe had to have her *now*. But her hands didn't seem to know what to do now that she'd come, fluttering from his neck to shoulders to neck again. Gabe ached with the need for her do more. "Touch me."

Her entire body went rigid, and he only had half a second to wonder if he'd said something wrong before she shrieked.

• • •

The guy in bed with her was not Nathan.

Which meant Elle was buck-naked and wantonly riding the wrong guy.

She scrambled away from him and immediately fell off the bed. He hadn't sounded quite right when he asked if this was okay, but Elle had been too focused on not embarrassing herself to worry about how he sounded just then—he had been asleep, after all, and why would there be another guy in Nathan's bed?— but there was no mistaking the difference in his voice now.

She needed to catch her breath, but she could hear him moving closer to where she'd landed in a heap. "Babe, what's wrong?"

Babe? She scrambled to the wall and flailed for the light switch. When the lights clicked on, it was everything she could do to not hyperventilate. "*Oh my God.*"

How could she have mistaken that man for Nathan? Sure, they had freakishly similar bodies—or at least what she pictured Nathan's body would look like—and similar hair, but this man had *tattoos*. Elle nearly whimpered at the sight of so much ink. Even from this distance, she could tell it was really well done—more artwork than branding. Good God, he practically had a neon sign over his head that screamed "Bad Boy."

He was exactly the type of man she would

have chosen for herself.

Making him exactly the type of man she'd vowed to avoid at any cost. And she'd almost slept with him.

Oh God, oh God, oh God. A thick band tightened around her chest, making it impossible to catch a full breath. Spots danced over her vision as she fought to inhale. She was going to die right here in Nathan's loft. They'd find her naked body and that's what she'd be known as until the end of time—the woman who died in the middle of a botched seduction of the wrong man. Her mother would bring her back from the dead just to kill her for the embarrassment to the family.

Elle swayed, smacking into the wall with her back. Not enough air. She clawed at her chest, desperate for oxygen. A hand grabbed her chin, forcing her to look into gorgeous brown eyes. "Breathe, babe. Big inhale, hold it, now exhale."

Air rushed into her lungs, so much it made her light-headed. Elle shuddered at the strength of his fingers digging into her jaw. It didn't hurt, but there was no mistaking the possibilities they held. Heck, hadn't she seen that all too well just five minutes ago? "Get away from me," she wheezed, smacking his hands away.

He let go of her, but he didn't move back nearly enough. "What's wrong?"

What was wrong? *Everything* was wrong. Right about now she was supposed to be making love to Nathan, not standing naked in front of a stranger. His gaze flicked over her chest and she immediately tried to cover her breasts with her hands. "This isn't happening."

Maybe this was all a fever dream. That had to be it. She was probably safely tucked away in her bed, tossing and turning and twisting up the sheets. Elle closed her eyes and then opened them again. That too-masculine face still dominated her vision, perfectly shaped lips turning down in a frown. Why was she noticing his lips? "Oh God, this *is* happening."

The guy crossed his arms over his chest, which only served to remind her that he was naked. Against her will, her eyes skated down his nicely muscled torso and got stuck right around his hips. It didn't help that he was still aroused.

Time to go, Elle.

"Wait." He reached for her again, but she scrambled back, desperate to stay out of reach. God only knew what would happen if she had his hands on her again. "Please don't go."

The man held out his arms as if he were

trying to calm a skittish horse. Elle didn't like that mental comparison. At all. She started sliding sideways away from him. "This was a mistake. A terrible mistake." And she had to get out of there.

"Like hell it was."

She snatched up her lingerie then changed her mind, tossing it on the floor and grabbing the sheet he'd kicked off the bed. She wrapped it around her body. "You know what? It doesn't matter. Right? Right."

"It might help if you told me what's going on."

Elle forced her gaze back to his face. *What's going on?* It felt pretty obvious to her. She'd almost had sex with a stranger. If he hadn't said anything, she would have. Her breathing got all choppy again just thinking about the implications. "You're not Nathan," she choked out.

He dropped heavily onto the bed, emotions flickering over his face. Shock. Horror. Guilt. Something that might be regret.

She pressed her fingers to her mouth. "I have to go. I'm sorry." And then she fled, closing the door softly behind her.

CHAPTER TWO

You're not Nathan.

A terrible idea had blossomed in his mind the second the words left that gorgeous mouth of hers. He hadn't just hooked up with his brother's girlfriend, had he? Christ, he'd even *liked* it. This was not okay.

Gabe bolted off the bed. No way was she getting away that easily. Not without some sort of explanation. He pulled on his pants and threw open the door.

The loft, of course, was empty.

Ignoring the little voice inside demanding he give up and crawl back into bed, he marched to the other bedroom and banged on the door. "You better be goddamned decent, Nathan." When his little brother grumbled a response, Gabe strode into the room. "Get up."

Nathan burrowed under one of the five pillows on his bed. "Go away."

Gabe yanked off his blanket and smacked him on the back. "Up."

"What the hell?" He lifted his head long enough to look at the digital clock on his nightstand. "Why am I awake at this ungodly hour?"

"You aren't dating anyone, are you?" It was a long shot with Nathan's history, but he'd never forgive himself if he'd nearly banged his brother's girlfriend.

"What? No. Where would you get an idea like that?"

"You know a blonde? Gorgeous, rockin' body, about yea high?" He held his hand up to his shoulder.

Nathan sat up and ran his hands over his face. "Could be a number of women I know."

"This one would be nursing a thing for you."

His little brother cringed. "My coordinator, Elle. Sweet girl, really nice—innocent even. She's been throwing hints like crazy that she wants me to ask her out, but it's just not there for me."

Sweet. Nice. While those words might work, Gabe didn't believe the innocent part. She might be mostly a good girl, but good girls didn't crawl into bed intent on seducing a man. Then again, what did he know? Gabe didn't make a habit of associating with good girls.

"Elle." He liked the way her name rolled off his tongue, though. Hell, he'd like to roll more than that off his tongue.

"Why are you asking?"

He considered lying, but he'd never get away with it. Especially with his brother. "You swear you don't want her?"

"I would tell if you if I did." Nathan narrowed his eyes. "What's going on?"

Gabe took a deep breath and told him everything. When he finished, Nathan was laughing so hard his face turned a mottled shade of red. Seeing the horrified look on Elle's face all over again, the perfect "o" of her pink lips when she'd turned on the light and got a look at him, Gabe barely resisted punching something— preferably his idiot brother's face. "I don't see what's so goddamn hilarious."

"Only you. This would only happen to you." Nathan made an effort to be serious, but he couldn't seem to stop grinning. "I never would have guessed she had a scheme like this in her. I'm actually kind of impressed."

"Ha ha ha. So funny she freaked out in the middle of it, and ran off without even getting dressed first." Gabe ran a hand through his hair and sat heavily on the side of Nathan's bed. "Hell, man, she took your sheet."

That sobered his brother up. "If she quits because of this, I'm not going to be happy."

So it wasn't just the loss of his 1,500-thread-count sheets that wiped the smile off his brother's face. "None of this is my goddamn fault."

Nathan frowned. "You're more pissed about this than I'd expect."

Despite being the younger brother, he'd always been overprotective of Gabe. They were all each other had. But that didn't mean he wanted to get into the mushy stuff or explain how much it hurt to have Elle literally run from him after the glimpse of heaven she'd given him. "I just… She's different."

"Yes, she is, which is why I'm not going to be happy if she quits." Nathan sighed and climbed out of bed. "Don't suppose you started coffee before bursting in here? Because obviously I'm not getting any more sleep tonight."

"Nope."

"Sadist."

"You act like you're surprised." Gabe followed

him into the kitchen and grabbed a stool.

They both watched the coffee fill the pot, one drip at a time. It was only when he'd poured two cups that Nathan finally said, "It's good to have you back."

Gabe had been gone longer than normal this time around. It wasn't planned, but everything that could go wrong had with the L.A. club. "It's good to be home." Or it had been until Elle climbed into his bed and then acted like she'd kissed a monster. Not exactly the most encouraging response.

As they drank their coffee, Gabe watched his brother. Nathan looked like shit. Oh, not that the average person would notice, but Gabe was family—he knew when something was wrong with his brother. It had been like this for a long time, but things seemed to be worse every time he came home. "How you doing?"

Nathan shrugged, just like he always did. "Fine. Working on something new and it's kicking my ass."

Gabe had the sneaking suspicion the source of his little brother's demons was a woman from their past, but they never talked about it. "You say that, and then it ends up selling for a shit-ton of money."

"I'm good at what I do." He finally grinned. "So how was L.A.? Took your ass long enough to get back here."

"It was a mess. The G.M. I hired had a thing for pretty redheaded bartenders with more tits than sense, and he was skimming off the top. I finally had to fire the whole lot of them." A month. A whole damn month to find a decent replacement. "But I found a chick who knows her stuff. Lynn doesn't take shit from anyone." Gabe needed a ballbuster to keep all those high-strung bartenders in line.

"How long you sticking around this time?"

"No idea. I'm going to need to visit the rest of the clubs soon—make sure things are running smoothly. You know, the usual." He tried to do a tour of the clubs he owned at least two or three times a year. It was too easy for things to slip under the radar when he wasn't around. Then again, he might actually have a new reason to stick around Spokane now. "So tell me about Elle."

Nathan set his cup down. "Like I said, she's a good girl. Works hard, though I don't know much about her private life. I served with her brother in Iraq. He's a good guy, a better soldier. I can tell you right now Ian won't like you sniffing around his precious little sister."

What big brother would? Gabe wasn't exactly the kind of man women took home to meet their parents. He had the hard life written all over him, from the way he carried himself to the ink on his skin. Always had. The thought made him want to snarl. "She's the one who started this."

"Hey, I'm not arguing with you. All I'm asking is, how far do you plan on taking it?"

It was something he hadn't considered. Gabe took a drink of the cooling coffee. There were too many variables to say for sure. All he knew was that he didn't want his last sight of Elle to be her fleeing from him. "I don't know, but I want to find out."

"Then I suppose you'll need to ask her out."

Again, the look on her face appeared in his head. "I doubt she'd say yes."

"And when has a little thing like 'no' stood in the way of your goal?"

If Gabe were put off by rejection, he never would have gotten their first nightclub off the ground, inherited money or no. Hell, even if he'd been able to start that first club, there wouldn't be clubs in all the major West Coast cities. He grinned. "A good point, little brother, a very good point."

• • •

Oh my God, oh my God, oh my God. Elle kept up a steady mental chant as she drove home, barely seeing the road in front of her. "That didn't happen. There's no way that happened." She shook her head even as every part of her body proclaimed the truth. Not only did she orgasm so hard she'd seen stars, but she'd done it with the *wrong man*.

How the heck hadn't she noticed the guy she was kissing wasn't freaking Nathan? Oh wait, probably because the way his mouth seemed to brand her as *his* made Elle's toes curl and her thoughts short out. It was like the plot of a daytime soap opera, right up there with sleeping with the wrong twin. Stuff like that wasn't supposed to happen in real life. It was fiction, too far-fetched to ever be believable. The kind of thing people like Elle rolled their eyes at.

And yet here she was. Apparently stuff like this actually did happen in real life.

It wasn't her fault, she reasoned. Their bodies weren't that different, what with those wide shoulders and slightly too-long hair. Sure, the stranger had more bulk than Nathan, but how was she supposed to know what he may or may not have been hiding underneath his dress shirts and slacks? There was that same wicked curl of their lips, too. Really, anyone would have made the same mistake. It didn't help that she'd lost her mind as soon as he touched her.

But he didn't look all that much like Nathan in the cold light of day. The man was all marked up, with half of his torso covered in tattoos. Really, really sexy tattoos—

No. She couldn't afford to think like that. Not *again*. Not when the guy she'd almost slept with reminded her so much of her miserable excuse for an ex.

She shuddered. She'd been fresh out of high school, and it was so easy to be pulled in by his bad-boy looks and charming smile. And things had gone great…right up to the point where she finally agreed to have sex with him. After he'd jumped the hurdle that was her virginity, it had taken all of forty-eight hours for him to turn around and dump her.

Her ex, Jason, was the reason she'd picked Nathan. He wasn't the type to sleep around, and her sanity wasn't swept away whenever they were in the same room together. Nathan was safe. Unlike the stranger in his loft. Where Nathan was refined and classy, this other guy was a bad boy from his rough looks to his brown eyes that seemed to drink her up. Elle shivered.

Why was he even there? In the master bedroom, no less. Nathan never had company, and even if he did, there was a guest room—

She startled so hard, she nearly drove off the road. What if he was Nathan's lover? She hadn't seen her boss with a woman the entire year she'd worked for him, and Elle had just assumed that it was because he was a decent man who didn't jump from bed to bed. What if the reason she'd never seen a woman was because he didn't swing that way?

The thought made her breath come in short gasps. Oh God, what if her mother found out about this? Elle would never hear the end of it. Not only had she gotten naked with the wrong man, but the man she'd been aiming for might not even like women.

Except, if that guy was sleeping with her boss, why wasn't Nathan in bed with him? His car had been in the parking lot, so he should've been there. And the stranger…he'd been kind of into what they'd been doing. Or at least she thought so. Then again, she'd already proven her radar for these things was seriously broken. But she was pretty darn sure he wouldn't have done what he did if he wasn't attracted to her. Maybe he just felt sorry for her?

Lord, she was spiraling. Roxanne would know what to think of this. Her phone lay on top of her purse on the seat next to her, a silent reminder that she'd promised to call her best friend. Elle couldn't do it. Roxanne had said this plan was a horrible idea from the start—she wouldn't be able to stop from saying "I told you so" and, right now, that was the last thing Elle needed to hear. No, Roxanne could wait until their Monday coffee for her update.

The completely irrational urge to call her mother came over her, but Elle killed it. She'd made the mistake of going to her mom after the disaster with Jason, and Elle had been regretting it ever since.

The rest of the night stretched before her, hours full of nothing to do but stress out and kick herself for getting into this mess in the first place. She should have asked Nathan out like a normal person, instead of trying to force his hand. But what was she supposed to do? Her mother kept strong-arming her into dinner after dinner with dull men—for her own good, of course—and Elle had been desperate to pick someone suitable for herself. At least she could spend time with Nathan without being tempted to escape out a bathroom window.

She turned into her driveway and glanced around. The street was empty, it being too late for most people to be out and about. She could definitely make it to her front door without anyone seeing. Piece of cake.

Tucking the sheet more tightly around her chest and buttoning up her coat, she climbed out of the car and hurried to the front door. Once inside—and away from prying eyes—she sank to the floor and curled into a ball. "This is my life." How pathetic. Elle inhaled, fighting for control, but all she got was the spicy smell of the guy she'd almost slept with. She bolted upright. *Oh God.* "And I don't even know his name."

Then she burst into tears. Scrambling to get out of her coat and the sheet, she pushed to her feet and stumbled up the stairs. With every step, she got a face full of his scent. She could still feel his hands on her, calloused palms sending shivers through her entire body. And his mouth…good God, the man's mouth on her breasts alone had nearly been enough to send her over the edge.

Elle slammed open her bedroom door and rushed into the bathroom. Without waiting for the water to heat up, she stepped in and reached for her body wash and pouf. As quickly as possible, she lathered up and scrubbed her skin, desperate to remove every reminder of last night. No matter how hard she scrubbed, though, she couldn't erase the memory of his fingers inside her, his lips on hers, his arms holding her close. As if she actually mattered to him. They were complete strangers. What a horrid joke.

She'd apologized to him, she realized. On her way out the door, she'd actually *apologized*. Indignation cut through the edges of her misery. Why had she apologized? This wasn't *her* fault. He was the one who let her make a fool of herself. A man with any sort of morals—no matter how dangerously attractive—would've put a stop to her botched seduction the second she slipped into his bed.

Which was just further proof that Elle had awful taste in men.

She ducked her head under the spray and stayed like that for a long time, very carefully not thinking about anything but the way the water seemed to cleanse her, washing away the lingering panic. She refused to think about how good the man had made her feel. How her body still throbbed with latent desire.

Elle got out of the shower, dried off, and threw on an oversize shirt. There was only one thing that would make her even a little bit better right now.

She hurried into the spare bedroom that she'd converted into a studio and yanked out a spare canvas. Forcing herself to slow down, she picked up her palette and started with wide, sweeping strokes, laying the background that the final picture would ultimately emerge from. After picking out one of her favorite stock photos—a gorgeous shirtless man with washboard abs— she flipped on her favorite mix of classical music. Slowly, oh so slowly, the tension left her muscles as she started in on the subject itself.

Everything would be okay. It had to be. With a deep breath, Elle gave herself over to painting, letting herself relax into it. For a time, there were only the motions of dipping her brush, of stroking it over the canvas, of blending the colors together.

The painting evolved slowly, forming into a man's bare chest. It was a nice chest, with wide shoulders that tapered down to a narrow waist. Not a swimmer's body like the man in her stock photo, though—there was too much bulk in the muscles for that kind of lean strength.

She blinked. Why did that chest look so

familiar?

The realization dawned on her, nightmarishly slow. Oh God, it was *him*.

With a shriek, she flung her brush across the room. This was ridiculous. It was everything she could do not to haul the painting out back and take a blowtorch to the canvas. Elle grabbed one of the spare sheets she kept to cover the carpet. With careful, concise motions, she draped it over the canvas, turned, and walked out of the room, shutting the door softly behind her.

Last night happened. It was over. Soon, she'd have to face the consequences. But not yet. Tomorrow was another day and she'd deal with it then.

Despite her pep talk, the memories still swarmed on the edge of her consciousness, circling like sharks scenting blood in the water, waiting for one more misstep to tear her to pieces.

CHAPTER THREE

"You did *what*?"

Without looking up, Elle systematically shredded her napkin. It gave her something to focus on besides the incredulous brunette across the table. "You know—what we talked about."

"You slept with—" Roxanne looked around and lowered her voice. "You slept with Nathan?"

She could have yelled it to the heavens—there was no one in the coffee shop but Marge, and the old woman was half deaf. Elle resumed her shredding, tearing the strips into neat little squares. "No."

"Oh, thank God. For a second there I'd thought you'd lost your mind and actually gone through with it."

Elle forced herself to meet Roxanne's green

eyes. She'd always thought they were so much more exotic than her basic blue ones. And, yes, she was most definitely stalling. "I didn't sleep with Nathan… I mean, I almost did. Except… whoever it was that I climbed into bed with, he wasn't Nathan."

Thinking about it again had anger curdling in her stomach. After her botched attempt to paint, an entire day spent scrubbing her house from top to bottom still hadn't helped the knowledge sit any easier. Not only had she not recognized that the man she was intimate with wasn't Nathan, she had *enjoyed* it. And that was just freaking unacceptable.

It wasn't her fault, though. She was sticking to her guns on that point. There's no way she could have known it wasn't Nathan touching her and setting her body on fire. She'd even whispered his name before crawling into bed and he'd answered, for God's sake. Okay, she'd been really quiet and he'd kind of sighed in response, but she'd done her due diligence. He should've stopped her the second she touched him.

Yes, this was most definitely *his* fault.

As much as she liked this revelation, she hated that her treacherous body reacted every time she so much as pictured his face. It had all felt so good while she was doing it that she wondered how good actual sex would have been—which was, again, *freaking unacceptable*.

Roxanne paled beneath her perfect tan. "Honey, I think you'd better go back to the beginning and try that again."

She really, really didn't want to, but there was no arguing with the look on her friend's face. "Nathan made a comment about working on a new design this weekend, so I figured it was the perfect time. I even went out and bought" —she lowered her voice— "*lingerie.*" That she'd left behind. Elle's face heated. She was no better than Cinderella leaving her glass slipper at the ball like a calling card. There'd be no way to keep Nathan from finding out about this. Yet another unforgivable sin to lay at the stranger's feet.

"Moving right along…"

Might as well get her humiliation out in the open. Elle took a gulp of her latte and nearly choked on the too-hot liquid. Okay, not the greatest idea she ever had. Then again, neither was Saturday night. "I…seduced him. Or something. Either way, we ended up in bed together. I thought it was Nathan." And it'd been amazing. Beyond amazing. Her thighs clenched at the memory of how it felt when Nathan— But it wasn't Nathan.

"It was a freaking stranger and that…that…*asshole* almost let me sleep with him."

Roxanne blinked. "Am I mistaken or did an honest-to-God curse word just come out of your mouth?"

But Elle was too focused on her problems to worry about swearing. How was she going to face Nathan? What if he brought it up? Oh lord. Today was going to be H-E-double-hockey-sticks. God, what if he already knew and fired her because of it? The gallery was her life. She couldn't lose it. "I think I'm going to die of embarrassment. That's possible, right? It's got to be because it's happening right now."

"You're just being dramatic. So, what happened? If it wasn't Nathan, who did you get into bed with?" She frowned. "And just how did you manage to do it without realizing he was the wrong guy?"

"It was dark in the room."

"Uh huh. There's this neat little thing called a light switch. You should try it sometime."

"It seemed easier that way." It sounded stupid to say it aloud, but it was the truth. If Nathan was going to reject her, she didn't want to see his face—or let him see her nearly naked—while he did it.

"It was so easy, you jumped the wrong guy." She sat back when Elle flinched, covering her mouth with a hand. "Sorry. It just slipped out."

"It's okay. Maybe we can even laugh about this in like, oh, fifteen years." Not right now, though. It was too soon. Heck, she could still feel the imprint of him against her body. What kind of man let a strange woman climb into his bed anyway? He should've stopped her!

Elle shook her head. Spending any more time obsessing over that night would get her nowhere. It was time to move on with her life—and figure out how she was going to do damage control. "Whoever the guy was, he's probably just a friend who slept over. I've never seen him before." And hopefully she'd never see him again.

"I'm sure you're right." Roxanne smiled, but it was her Party Planner Smile—brighter than the sun and fake as all get-out. "What are you going to do about Nathan?"

The question of the hour. Elle pictured the long lines of his face, completely arresting pale blue eyes, blondish hair just long enough to give him a rakish look without losing his cultured aura. The image blurred, replaced by the stranger from Saturday night. He wasn't refined at all, between the tattoos, the muscles, and the nose that had obviously been broken more than once. He was exactly the opposite of everything she needed in a man—the type of man she'd already learned wasn't the keeping kind. Hadn't her mother said the very same thing when Elle confided in her about Jason? She'd been right then, and she was right now.

When Elle said as much, Roxanne rolled her eyes. "Oh please. Your mom likes the sound of her voice too much. She doesn't know what you need."

Sure, her mom had been seriously misguided in some of her picks, but they were all respectable, upstanding citizens. Men who would take care of a woman and their future brood of children. Men who wouldn't leave Elle crying and brokenhearted. "You're wrong. This guy is bad news." He'd have to be for Elle to want him so much.

A voice inside her whispered that Nathan wouldn't let a drug kingpin spend the night in his loft, but Elle smothered it. She dredged up a fake smile of her own. "And, to answer your question, nothing happens with Nathan. Heck, he's probably gay and that guy was his lover or something. I'm just going to forget it ever happened."

"Be sure to let me know how that works

out." Roxanne gave her hand another pat and sipped her iced quad-shot mocha. How she managed to drink those without having a heart attack was a mystery. "You know, there's part of me that wants to say 'I told you so,' but it seems in really bad taste." She set down her cup and frowned. "Even I didn't see it turning out like this. Well-played on that part."

"*Roxanne.*"

"What? I'm actually impressed—horrified, but impressed. Nathan's not gay, by the way. One of my friends—female friends—dated him a few years back. But that's neither here nor there." She leaned in again, tapping her perfectly manicured nails on the tabletop. "So...how far did you get before you realized he wasn't Nathan?"

"Far enough."

Roxanne's green eyes lit up. "That sounds promising. Was he any good?"

Good didn't begin to cover it. Elle had never felt so much, had never known it could be like that, but it was too embarrassing to admit aloud she'd actually enjoyed herself, even to Roxanne. "I'm not talking about this."

Roxanne drummed her fingernails along the table again, drawing Elle back to the present.

"How am I supposed to live vicariously through your mistakes if you don't talk about it?"

"You aren't." Elle grabbed her purse and dug through it until she found her wallet. Tossing a ten on the table, she stood. "I have to get going if I don't want to be late." Even though she'd rather do anything other than go into work this morning.

"We will talk about this, even if I have to hog-tie you to do it." Roxanne pushed to her feet. Impossible to imagine her hog-tying anyone in a pencil skirt, but Elle had seen how she was when she decided on a goal. Roxanne was unstoppable and God help anyone who got in her way.

"I just need time to process it all." Hopefully if she stalled long enough, Roxanne would let it go.

Engulfing Elle in an ocean-scented hug, she laughed. "Stall all you like, but once I get a few martinis in you, you'll share. Next Friday is girls' night out, remember?"

Crap. The worst part was that she was right. Elle couldn't hold her liquor. Last time they went out, Roxanne had dragged her to karaoke, promising that they were just going to grab a booth and watch. Two martinis in and Elle decided she was a rock star and sang "Take It

Off." She was still trying to live that down.

"Don't worry, we won't do karaoke this time." Roxanne went on, a terrifyingly innocent smile on her face. "I'll find somewhere nice and quiet where you can share all the juicy details."

Elle resolved to keep herself to a one-martini limit, and to turn Friday night's conversation to Roxanne's party planning job. The woman was downright terrifying in her pursuit of making sure everything went off perfectly. "Sounds great."

"You're a terrible liar, but that's okay. It's part of the reason I adore you so much." She air-kissed Elle's cheeks and sailed out the door.

Shaking her head, Elle hiked her purse higher onto her shoulder and headed for the gallery a couple blocks away. Even so early in the morning, the sky was clear and a warm blue that only seemed to show up in the summer. She had half a mind to call in sick, head back to the parking garage, and drive out to one of the lakes in the area. Lying on a towel, listening to the boats cruise by, sounded significantly more attractive than facing Nathan.

But she refused to be a coward. Elle loved everything about her job. Nathan was a dream boss, and being surrounded by art she felt so passionately about was heaven. Maybe Roxanne was right and she shouldn't have tried to mix business with pleasure, but there was no point in worrying about it now. Thanks to her screwup, she wouldn't have to deal with balancing a potential relationship with work, because Nathan would never think of her as the kind of respectable woman he'd like to date once he found out.

Shoulders sagging, she pulled out her keys and stopped in front of the huge windows of the gallery. The muted underwater scenes had been replaced by a series she'd never seen before. Moving closer to the glass, she studied the paintings. They were startlingly bleak, depicting scenes she recognized from Dante's *Inferno*. Elle had never liked that particular work, but she couldn't deny that the pieces Nathan had picked were compelling even as they made her want to look away.

The door opened, and the man himself stepped onto the sidewalk. Elle tried to focus on Nathan, but her attention kept straying to the center painting—the one showing the second circle of hell. There was a couple in the forefront, both naked though it was hard to tell with the way the wind whipped their hair over their bodies. They reached for each other, desperation written over their entire beings, fingertips missing contact by a scant breath of distance.

It was one of the most heartbreaking things she'd ever seen.

"What do you think?" The same question Nathan always asked her when he purchased something new.

Elle swallowed and peeked at him out of the corner of her eye, wondering if he knew what happened on Saturday night. Surely he'd say something? Because, as bad as it was that she'd almost had sex with one of his friends—or, God forbid, his lover—it'd be even worse if Nathan knew. There'd be no way to hide the fact she'd been trying to have sex with *him*.

But he was completely focused on the painting. Okay, she could do this. "I didn't know you were picking up a new artist."

"I didn't know I was either." He laughed. "But I stumbled across these at a local art show and couldn't resist."

She studied the tone of his voice and came up empty. Nothing he said could be construed as anything other than exactly what he'd said. But she couldn't help continuing to examine him for any sign that he knew. When he only looked expectantly at her, obviously wanting her opinion on the paintings, she realized he had no idea what happened. There was no way he could know and still act so…Nathan.

Turning back to the painting, she said, "They're…" Terrifying. Beautiful. So very, very dark. "…intensely compelling."

His reflection in the glass met her gaze. "That's a pretty high compliment coming from you."

"You know I love everything you do." She realized what she just said and blushed. Maybe a hole would open up beneath her feet and swallow her. "I mean—um, you know what I mean."

"I do." Nathan laughed and took her elbow, leading her toward the door. "Come on. We have a lot to talk about with the gallery showing coming up."

Elle had a moment to wonder if her breakfast was going to come crawling out of her throat before he towed her through the door and into the gallery. It was okay, though, because Nathan clearly didn't know.

Her pulse quickened. If she got lucky, maybe he never would. Their cleaning service only came on Monday and Friday nights, so there was still time to sneak into the loft and grab her lingerie before they brought it to his attention tomorrow morning. She glanced at her watch. Only four hours to lunchtime—she'd sneak into the loft then. In the meantime, she could survive this morning.

Right?

CHAPTER FOUR

Gabe sat in his car, staring out at the street, and wondered if he'd lost his damn mind. This woman—Elle—didn't want anything to do with him. Hell, she'd practically run out of the room screaming when she realized he wasn't Nathan.

That said, he couldn't ignore how much he'd liked how it felt being with her. Elle was the polar opposite of the women he was used to. Her being so different should have turned him off—or at least just been a mild curiosity—but he couldn't shake the feeling that there could be more to this if he gave it a shot. Besides, Nathan thought ambushing her was a great idea.

He chose not to remember all of Nathan's other shit ideas that hadn't seemed so great once Gabe walked through the front door and into the gallery. There was a solid chance this one was shit as well. Christ, what was he thinking? She wasn't going to want to go out with him. He should just apologize and disappear from her life for good.

Yeah, that was a decent idea. Better than his first one. Plan in place, he meandered around the gallery. It'd been nearly six months since he'd been here last and Gabe was struck by his brother's collection, just like always. Though he wasn't an art snob by any means, there was no denying his brother had an eye for this stuff. Gabe still preferred the scrap-metal sculptures, but he could appreciate the chance Nathan gave to other artists whom he displayed in his galleries. No wonder the damn things sold for such insane prices.

"See something you like?"

He turned and was struck damn near dumb by the sight of Elle dressed in a funky pink skirt that showed off her killer legs and a striped tank top—a serious improvement over the ruffles and satin. *Yes.* Gabe definitely saw something he liked. A lot. Though her outfit wasn't overly clingy by any means, Gabe couldn't get the image of her naked out of his head. His cock jumped to attention despite his best effort.

"*You.*" Her blue eyes went wide and she

actually took a step back. "What are you doing here?"

Not exactly a warm welcome, but she wasn't calling the cops either. Gabe would take what he could get. "I came to buy a painting."

Elle. snorted— an accident if her blush was anything to go by. She ran her hands over her skirt, which distracted him all over again because it made the lines of her hips stand out. Gabe would give his left hand to be able to touch her there one more time.

"Stop it."

He jerked his gaze back to her face. "Stop what?" Would she actually accuse him of ogling her like a dirty old man?

"You—" Her eyes blazed, mouth drawn into a tight line before she smiled at him. Funny, she still looked pissed as hell despite the fact that her lips curved up. "Which piece were you considering?" Elle's tone said she doubted he could afford it.

The dismissive attitude stung his pride. This chick didn't know a damn thing about him. All she saw was the busted face and tattoos, and assumed he was trash. The truth was Gabe could buy every single painting in this goddamn gallery and still be sitting pretty.

Gritting his teeth, he turned toward the paintings near the front window, and played along. "These ones caught my eye."

He waited to see if she'd dismiss him, but Elle sighed and her heels clicked on the floor as she came over. "They're the newest available—they were just picked up from a show in town. Mr. Schultz has a passion for supporting local artists."

Mr. Schultz? Was she playing with him? Or did she really not realize he was Nathan's brother? Gabe watched her out of the corner of his eye, taking in the way she seemed to be unable to pull her gaze from the center one. "Are they a set?"

"They can be." Elle shrugged. "It's up to you if you want to spend the money to acquire them all." Again, her tone said she was humoring him. "They certainly seem to suit you."

Gabe recognized the theme as Dante's *Inferno*. Of course she'd think he was destined for one of the nine circles of hell. Inhaling deeply, he got caught up in the scent of her, something deep and woodsy. It wasn't a scent most women would choose, but it made his mouth water all the same. "And what would you choose?"

Elle blinked. "Me?"

"Yeah, you. You work here, so you must have

a favorite. Which one would you choose?"

"I don't see how that matters."

"Humor me." Gabe looked at the paintings. As usual, they ranged from the delicate and beautiful to completely abstract to the dark stuff behind him. No one could accuse his brother's taste of sticking to one niche—though they might have a case for multiple personality disorder. Which would she choose?

"You're serious?" When he just motioned for her to lead on, she huffed out a breath. "Fine."

Without hesitation, she marched through the gallery. Gabe followed, taking the opportunity to watch the play of muscle along the back of her legs. Those heels were killer. He definitely approved.

"Stop ogling me."

He found himself grinning. "Does it bother you?"

"Of course it bothers me. It's completely inappropriate." She waved at the painting she'd stopped in front of.

It was beautiful, which was hardly surprising. Pink flowers blossomed over stark black inkblots. It took him a second to place the background as a woman's back. Subtle, but it brought everything into focus.

"That would make a hell of a tattoo." He was already picking out the inks in his mind. The flowers would be difficult since they were so perfectly shaded, but Gabe could do it. He *wanted* to do it.

"Of course *you* would say that."

"What? You think tattoos aren't art? Just because it's ink and skin instead of paint and canvas doesn't make it any less of a masterpiece."

Even six inches shorter, she still managed to look down her nose at him. "What are you actually doing here?"

"I have no idea what you mean." Even as the lie rolled off his tongue, he got distracted with thoughts of kissing her. How could he not? The Cupid's bow was so inviting when she pursed her lips in disapproval.

She crossed her arms over her chest. "Are you really going to stand there and pretend like you're actually here to buy a painting?"

Someone had her panties in a twist. Gabe raised his eyebrows and feigned surprise. "What are you talking about?"

Her mouth did that "o" thing again. After a glance around as if making sure they were still alone, she leaned forward and poked his chest. "How dare you come to my place of work and act like you don't know who I am? This is all *your* fault."

Oh, this should be good. "How can you possibly blame me? I was in bed, minding my own damn business when *someone* decided they wanted some hanky-panky."

"Hanky-panky? What are you, twelve?" She poked him again, harder this time. "I thought you were Nathan the entire time. I didn't know who I was with. You knew I was a stranger and *you still would have had sex with me*."

He kind of liked this pissed-off side of her. "Well, yeah. I mean, look at you." He motioned to her, hoping if he kept talking she wouldn't call him on the crock of shit he was spinning. "What man is going to turn down a gorgeous, half-naked blonde crawling into bed with him? I may be pretty, but I'm not stupid."

"You—I swear—I can't believe you!"

Gabe decided he liked it when she sputtered even more. Then her gaze coasted over his body, the look so brief he never would have noticed it if he wasn't watching her so closely. He grinned. "Now I get it."

Her foot started tapping. Gabe could tell she was biting back words, but eventually her temper got the best of her. "Spit it out," she snapped.

"You *want* me. That's why you're so angry about this. You liked what we did. You wish we would've gone further."

"I do not!"

Yes, she had. Gabe had been around the block enough times to know when a woman was coming and when she was faking it, and Elle sure as hell hadn't been faking it. And, instead of flaunting what they'd done or flirting, she was wicked pissed. It turned him on. "Come out with me."

"Excuse me, what?"

"I want to take you on a date." Actually, he wanted to get her naked again, but Gabe could hardly say that out loud. She looked like she was going to spit in his face at the thought of sharing a meal together as it was.

"Absolutely not."

"There you are!"

They both turned as Nathan walked through the door. He smiled as if he hadn't overheard them arguing. "Elle, I see you've met my brother, Gabe."

For a second there, he thought her eyes were going to pop out of her head. "*Brother*?"

"Yep." He threw an arm around Gabe's shoulders. "He just got back into town Saturday night from dealing with one of his clubs in... where was it? San Francisco?"

"Los Angeles. San Francisco was last year." Which Nathan damn well knew. Any other chick would be panting at the thought of going on a date with him knowing he had multiple clubs—and the cash that went with them. Elle just looked like she'd swallowed something nasty.

"I didn't know you had a brother." She pressed her hand to her chest, and Gabe wondered if he was going to have to catch her when she passed out. But Elle took a deep breath and straightened, pasting a smile on her face. She shot Gabe a look, as if her boss's having a brother was his fault, too. "Pleasure to meet you."

"Yeah, you too." He couldn't decide if he liked this woman or if she drove him nuts—still too soon to tell. Hell, it might be both.

"I've got to go." Nathan gave Gabe another pat and headed for the door. "I've got a few appointments so I won't be back until well after lunch. Elle, take a couple hours off and lock up behind you." And then the bastard waltzed out the door.

Gabe didn't waste any time. "So about that date..."

With his brother gone, she let her anger rise

to her eyes again. "Not a chance."

No way was he going to let her get out of this. He shrugged, striving to appear unconcerned. "It's okay. I get it. You can barely look at me without wanting to toss me into a coat closet. It's no wonder you're hightailing it like a coward."

"You're insufferable! I'm no coward, and I most certainly do not want you."

He had her and she didn't even know it yet. "Prove it."

Her chin went up. "Fine. It's only lunch. What's the worst that could happen? Oh wait, it already did."

Okay, ouch. The woman had some claws. "Then you're safe."

"Hardly."

"How about I promise not to get you naked and ravish you?"

She started to say something, but bit it back at the last moment. The fire in her eyes nearly made him take back the promise.

Elle recovered quickly. "As if I would want your hands on me again. Been there, done that, bought a T-shirt. It wasn't that great."

Gabe started to point out that she sure as hell *did* enjoy their time together, but he swallowed the words. She'd agreed. Better get her in the car before she changed her mind. "Sounds great. I'll drive."

She hesitated and finally sighed. "Okay."

When he offered his hand, she pointedly ignored it and went to grab her purse instead. Well, fine. He led the way down the block and around the corner to where he'd parked.

"Oh my God." Elle actually laughed when he unlocked the door and held it open for her. "You are such a cliché."

Gabe looked from her to his red 1968 Camaro. It was in prime condition—he'd restored it himself, everything from the leather seats to the engine. "What are you talking about?"

"Nothing. Nothing at all." She slid into the passenger seat and Gabe shut the door, but he swore he heard her mutter, "I bet he has a leather jacket too."

Damn it, but he did.

CHAPTER FIVE

Elle watched the buildings fly by as Gabe drove away from downtown. What was she doing? Just because he pushed all her buttons and accused her of being attracted to him didn't mean she had to actually go to lunch with the man. But she'd gotten so freaking *angry* when he smirked at her. As if he had women crawling into his bed every night. Heck, maybe he did. She clenched her fists, nails digging into her palms.

But, darn it, the fool man was right. She *had* been checking him out. Seriously, though, who could blame her? He might be an arrogant a-hole, but being in the same room as him made her body hum in anticipation. She knew all too well how good his skin felt against hers.

No. She wasn't going to think like that. Elle

shifted, wrapping her arms around herself. This car was really too small for comfort. Seriously, there was a mere six inches separating them and she could *smell* him—or his cologne or whatever. Not to mention that every time he shifted gears, his elbow brushed her arm, sending waves of warmth through her. Betraying heat started between her legs as memories swamped her. Good lord, he'd had magic hands. She'd never felt like that before.

Enough was enough. "Can you turn on the AC or something?"

He glanced at her long enough to raise his eyebrows. "This car doesn't have AC."

Of course it didn't. Why would this Neanderthal invest in something so basic? She recrossed her arms and fought not to slouch. "Then open a window or something."

He laughed. "Babe, I have crank windows."

It was like God hated her. She leaned forward and muscled the window down. As soon as the breeze hit her face, she could breathe again. Elle closed her eyes and strove for calm. She could do this. It was only one lunch. It wasn't like she was marrying the guy.

What a nightmare *that* would be.

"Don't call me babe. I'm not a floozy. Or a

freaking talking pig."

For a long moment, she hoped he would just let the silence stretch out between them. She wasn't that lucky.

"You weren't this pissy the other night."

Elle dug her fingernails into her palm so hard, she was surprised she didn't draw blood. She was in serious danger of losing her temper if she didn't calm down. When she spoke, she clipped her words in an effort to avoid screaming at him. "Let's get one thing straight—that was a mistake. A really stupid mistake. And we are never going to speak of it again."

"You think so?"

Which part? She refused to ask him to clarify. "Yes."

"Then I suppose I'll just have to change your mind."

Was there no deterring this guy? She was being downright rude and it didn't seem to faze him. She didn't get it. Gabe was the kind of guy who got around, she was sure of it, which meant wanting sex couldn't be the reason he was sniffing around her. He could, no doubt, get it anywhere. Sure, what they'd done had blown her mind, but it had to be pretty freaking tame compared to what he was used to. And as her ex-boyfriend had been so kind to point out, tame equaled boring. *About as sexy as fucking a corpse,* were the words Jason had used when he'd dumped her in front of all their friends.

Tears pricked her eyes, and she angrily blinked them away. Jason was an ass who'd used her just because he could, and cheated on her the entire time he was doing it. It was ridiculous that she kept hearing his voice in her head, picking away at her hard-won confidence. Just because she'd been down and darn near broken when he walked away didn't mean she was a loser. She might not be a porn star by night, or racy, or a wild child, but Elle had a lot going for her. Just because he didn't see it didn't mean someone else wouldn't—someone like Nathan. Except she hadn't seduced Nathan. She'd sneaked into bed with his *brother*.

Maybe she should just give up on men and join a nunnery.

"What is going on in that head of yours that's putting a frown on your face?"

"I'd make a terrible nun."

She hadn't meant to say that out loud, darn it. Gabe stared for so long, she made frantic motions for him to watch the road. "A nun?"

"Yes."

"I'm not going to pretend I'm familiar with nuns, but you, babe, are no freaking nun."

His words shouldn't have sent a thread of warmth through her, but they did. Clearly her hormones didn't care if he represented everything she'd sworn off in men—they just knew he made her feel good. Simple chemistry, even if it was annoying. It didn't matter. She could get through this.

"So how long have you worked for my brother?"

She sighed. Obviously they were going to force polite conversation, no matter how much she didn't want to. "About a year now."

"Do you like it?"

"Yes, of course." She frowned when Gabe laughed. "What's so funny?"

"Nothing. I just thought you'd be happier in one of those fancy museums in Seattle, rather than a little gallery here in town."

"Are you kidding?" She half-turned to face him. "It's the best job in the world. I spend every day surrounded by art, talking about art, buying and selling art. It's heaven."

Okay, wow, she hadn't meant to say so much. Usually when she started going off about her passion, people gave polite smiles and changed the subject.

Gabe just grinned. "I know what you mean."

She didn't see how he could know what she meant. Nathan was the cultured one. The artist. This man was as opposite from his brother as two people could be. He didn't say anything else, though, which left their conversation in an odd lull. Elle turned to the open window and hoped he'd get the hint.

Thankfully, Gabe did. They spent the rest of the ride in silence. It wasn't until he pulled into a gravel parking lot that she actually looked at the building. "You've got to be joking."

"What?" Bless his heart, he actually seemed baffled.

"I'm not going in there." As if the parking lot wasn't bad enough, the peeling paint and bars on the window were more than enough to convince her this was a terrible idea. Bars on the freaking window. Elle had never been in a restaurant that needed something like that, and she didn't want to start now.

"Lou's has the best burgers in town."

"I don't care. I have no plans for getting shot today."

Gabe actually had the audacity to laugh at her. "You're being dramatic." He got out of the car before she stopped sputtering and lumbered around to open her door. "Here's the deal—we're here, so I'm eating. You can sit in the car and wait for me, or you can come in and enjoy a burger. Your choice."

It wasn't a choice and he darn well knew it. The only thing worse than going into that heap was sitting in the parking lot alone. God only knew what could happen to her out here. Elle clutched her purse to her chest and climbed out of the car, telling herself it was only lunch. She could get through one meal without throwing something at his smug face. Really, she could.

Elle followed Gabe into the pub, stopping just inside the door to let her eyes adjust to the gloom. Holy crap, she was going to get hepatitis just from sitting in one of these booths. Maybe waiting in the car wasn't such a bad idea. Before she could back out the door, Gabe grabbed her hand and towed her through the room. It was empty but for three older men at one side of the bar and a group of women at the opposite end.

The men were the types she imagined frequented trashy bars across the world: backs bent and clothes worn from a lifetime of hard work. The women were apparently workers of another nature. No, that wasn't fair. She shouldn't judge people on how they were dressed, but who in the heck hung out in a place like this wearing miniskirts and six-inch heels? Not to mention the intense amount of makeup. Elle checked her watch to make sure she hadn't blacked out or time-traveled—yep, it was still only noon.

Gabe gave her a little push into a booth in the back of the room, and she cringed at the way the tears in the fake leather scratched the back of her legs as she slid over. This might actually be a new low point in her life. Goody.

The bartender didn't even come to their table. He just leaned over the bar and yelled, "Whaddya want?"

"Two burgers, a Bud, and…" He glanced at her.

"A Diet Coke."

"A Diet Coke," Gabe finished.

"Got it." The bartender disappeared through a doorway leading off the bar. Either he was taking in their order or, if his voice was any indication, going off for a smoke break. "Heck, maybe he's going to Narnia."

"What?"

Crap, she hadn't meant to say that out loud either. "I cannot believe you brought me here."

"What's wrong with here?" Gabe looked around as if he couldn't figure out what the problem was. No surprise there. He no doubt frequented places like this. It would never cross his mind that she wouldn't be comfortable. Yet another reason her night with him was one giant check in the mistake column.

She shifted, trying to keep the tear in the seat from digging into her thighs. It might have worked if the entire seat weren't covered in tears. And, seriously, she didn't even want to know what was making it sticky. Elle was going to need a bleach bath after this.

The bartender reappeared before things could get even more awkward, bringing two plates of burgers and fries. At least they looked edible, which was more than she'd been expecting. The faster she ate, the faster she could get out of this place and back to the gallery.

CHAPTER SIX

Gabe watched Elle pick at her food. He started to make a joke, but choked the words back at last second. He was pretty damn sure she wanted to stab him through the eye with the fork in her hand and, from the expression on her face, she might actually believe it if he said the burger was made from dog meat. She was a bit green around the gills already, but of course she was too much of a lady to say so. Instead, she started eating the french fries…with a fork.

He froze for a second, wondering if she expected him to eat in the same way. Gabe wasn't used to feeling so awkward. Maybe he should have taken her someplace ritzy or something, but he wasn't comfortable in those places. Never had been. Most of the women he'd taken out before would be perfectly at home in Lou's—and they wouldn't be drinking Diet Coke.

But none of those women had made him think about waking up next to them on a regular basis. He'd obviously lost his mind.

Yet again, he wondered if this really was a shitty mistake.

They ate in silence for a while before he couldn't stand it any longer. "So, are you from around here?"

Elle gave him a look that would have peeled paint before she shrugged. "I grew up just outside of town. My parents own a farm in Greenbluff."

So she was a country girl. No wonder she turned out so good. Probably came from one of those perfect families, too, where the father never drank too much and took it out on his kids, and the mother was always there to read to them before she tucked them into bed.

Bitterness soured the taste of burger in his mouth. Growing up hadn't been a fairy tale—not by a long shot—but it didn't matter anymore. He and Nathan got out, went on to make something of themselves. They were just as good as this country corn princess sitting across from him.

"Are you okay?"

He blinked. Had she already asked him that?

Gabe took another bite of his burger, hoping it would drown out the ugliness inside him threatening to rise to the surface. "Fine."

Elle squirmed, making the seat under her squeak. "What about you? Do you live in Spokane?"

It must have cost her to ask when she obviously wanted to be anywhere but here. Crazy how deeply ingrained those manners must be. Gabe swallowed his bite, wondering if he should lay his history out there. No. Better not. If she looked at him with pity in her eyes, he'd lose it. "Yeah, born and raised."

"Oh. Nice." She drank some more of her soda.

He hated how stilted this was. Gabe groped for something to say—something that didn't have to do with them rolling around naked together. She'd already proven she didn't want to even think about that anymore. Great. So what else was there?

"What do you do for fun?" He could kick himself for sounding like such a tool. Too late to take it back now, though.

She used her straw to stir the ice, around and around, until he was ready to snatch the damn thing out of her hands. Why did he bother asking? She probably volunteered at an animal shelter or took care of orphans or whatever else corn country princesses did. Hell, no doubt she was well on her way to sainthood.

"I…paint." The straw moved faster, as if she expected him to laugh at her.

"Paint?"

Elle's eyes flashed. "Yes, paint. It relaxes me. Most of the time."

And it was obviously a sore subject. But this one at least Gabe knew a little something about. He sat back and draped his arms over the top of the booth. "What medium do you use?"

"Watercolor, for the most part, though I've branched off a bit to ink."

"Ink, huh? So you don't mind getting those pretty hands dirty." Gabe took a swig of his beer and kept going before she had a chance to yell at him. "So what's your favorite subject?"

Her entire face went red despite the resolute expression on her face. "I don't have one."

He reached and laid his hand over the top of hers, stilling the straw's frantic movement. The touch brought back every memory of their night together—the taste of her, how her body squeezed his fingers when she came, the absolute perfection of her breasts —and he was suddenly very thankful of the tabletop hiding his lower body. Gabe cleared his throat. "Yes, you do."

"Are you calling me a liar?" Way too much anger there. Interesting.

"Apparently I am. Just tell me what you like to paint and I'll drop it." He had to know what got her so flustered. Maybe it wasn't fair, but as soon as she said she painted with watercolors, he figured she focused on flowers or landscapes or something equally ladylike.

Elle jerked her hand out from under his and grabbed the napkin from the table. Without looking up, she systematically shredded it into neat little columns. "I like painting men."

"Men."

"Stop judging me." Her hands moved faster as a pile of tiny squares started on the table. "It's not like they're nudes."

From the way her face went even redder, they obviously weren't fully clothed either. "So you lure these poor models into your home and make them strip so you can paint them?"

Elle gasped and the leftover pieces of napkins flew from her hands. "I never!"

"Do you want to?" He grinned, enjoying how flustered she was, her eyes darting over his face and chest. She already knew what it looked like and, from her quick inhale, Elle wasn't completely unaffected.

"No. I don't. That's completely inappropriate."

"You need some inappropriate in your life." Gabe decided he liked how outraged she was at the idea. He rubbed his forearm, noting how her gaze snagged on the tattoo he had there. "You like ink?" He'd thought a country corn princess like her would hate tattoos.

"Tattoos fascinate me," she said. The sour expression on her face told him she wasn't a fan of having to admit this, but he could practically feel her gaze caressing the design. Suddenly the phrase "like a moth to flame" made a whole lot more sense. "The good ones are so unique to the person who has them."

That's exactly what had drawn him to tats in the first place. Gabe turned his arm so she could see the full piece. "What do you think?" It was one he'd had done years ago by his mentor, and it looked as if his skin had been slashed away to reveal words beneath.

"The detail is exquisite. I've never seen anything quite like it." She cocked her head to the side, obviously intrigued despite herself. "What do the words say?"

Could it be? Elle was actually interested in something about him. Gabe loved tattoos more than damn near anything. If left unchecked, he could talk shop for hours. But never about *this* tattoo. He cleared his throat. "They're verses."

Another sharp glance. "By verses, you mean from the Bible?"

"Well, I'm not talking Van Halen."

"Ha ha. What verses are they?"

She sounded pretty damn grouchy, but Gabe didn't jump on the chance to make her more uncomfortable. Not when they were talking about *this* tattoo. Reluctantly, he said, "Hosea 11:9, Micah 7:7, Joshua 1:5, and Revelations 21:4."

"I'm not familiar with those."

"They're about hope. A whole lot of hope."

She raised her eyebrows. "I didn't peg you for a religious man."

Gabe forced himself to laugh, but it came out sounding hollow. "That's because I'm not. But these ones mean something to me regardless." They'd been his mother's favorites, the only thing she had to comfort herself at the end of the day. Raising two boys alone could do that to a woman. He shook his head, pushing back the memories.

She must have gotten the hint from the iciness in his tone, because Elle let it go. "Do all your tattoos mean something to you?" Bright curiosity shone from her eyes, a marked relief from her anger—no matter how sexy he found her when she was pissed. And, to be honest, Gabe was kind of thrilled that they had something in common. Twenty minutes ago, he wouldn't have believed it was possible.

"Of course. So, do you have any ink?"

Just like that, her anger was back. "Of course not. I'd never get a tattoo."

Interesting response considering how into ink she seemed to be. "Never say never, babe."

"You don't know anything about me."

He watched her while he finished off his burger. "Don't I? Because at this point, I know enough to make you scream the same way you did the other night." While she sputtered, her hands fluttering, he slid out of the booth. "Want to play some pool?"

"No, I most definitely do not."

How far could he push before she snapped and completely freaked out? Only one way to find out. "Same deal as before, babe. I'm playing—you can come with or hang out here by yourself."

"You're an ass."

"And you have a fantastic one." Gabe slid out of the booth and offered his hand. "Come on."

"As if I haven't heard *that* before." Her eyes flashed. "I want to go back to the gallery."

"There's plenty of time left before Nathan's back." He pulled out his cell phone. "You're more than welcome to call him and check if you want."

Elle stood, again ignoring his outstretched hand. This chick was going to give him a complex. It wasn't like he was crawling with infection or something. "I can't believe he just left me with you."

Best not to tell her this was Nathan's plan to begin with—or that his little brother knew about their night together and supported a repeat. "Look, I just want to spend a little more time with you. That's not so bad, is it?"

Elle bit her lip—Gabe was learning to both love and hate that move. "Right. Because our spending time together has worked so well in the past."

Apparently for all her sputtering, Ms. Country Corn Princess couldn't manage to get her mind out of the gutter. He liked that as much as he suspected she hated it. "If you have a better idea"—Gabe let his tone show just how dirty his thoughts were—"then I'm more than happy to hear it. Pick something. We'll do it."

"No, thanks. We can stick with pool."

He'd bet she'd have a different answer if it were Nathan asking her. But then, she actually wanted to spend time with his little brother. The only reason she was here right now was because of a *mistake*. Great. Now he was jealous of his little brother.

Scowling, Gabe led the way to the back of the bar where they had three pool tables set up. He put in two quarters and then set about racking the balls while Elle watched.

"I don't get you."

He switched the balls around, making sure they alternated between stripes and solids. "What's to get?"

"I—you know what? Never mind. Let's just play and get this over with."

He rolled over the white ball and nodded to the cue sticks behind her. "Go ahead and break."

"Why do I have to break?"

"Because I racked." He watched while she examined the sticks before finally picking one. "Want to make this interesting?"

"Interesting how, exactly?" She chalked up the tip and set about placing the cue ball.

He should just keep his mouth shut, but Gabe needed to get the picture of Elle and Nathan together out of his head. "A bet."

Elle leaned against the stick, her blond hair creating a halo in the dim lighting. She looked like an angel who'd accidentally wandered into hell. "I'm listening."

So she had a competitive streak. Good to know. "Classic eight ball. If I win, I get a kiss."

"God, you really are a cliché. No way."

"You don't get to make the terms. I want a kiss if I win. What do you want?"

Thoughts crossed her face, too many for him to pinpoint. Was that anger? Anticipation? Actual loathing? Finally Elle nodded. "Fine. You win, you get a kiss."

"A real one. Not some grade-school bullshit."

She rolled her eyes. "Fine. Whatever. You win, you get a real kiss. If I win, you promise you won't tell Nathan about what happened between us. You take me back to the gallery, and you leave me alone."

Gabe leaned against the wall, his hands in his front pockets. "You get one of those, not both. Unless I get to add to mine…"

"No, one's fine." She ran a hand over her skirt. "You don't tell Nathan. Do we have a deal?"

"Deal." Easy enough to promise—Nathan already knew. Guilt threatened to choke him, but

Gabe ignored it. As he'd quickly found out, playing this straight wasn't going to get him a chance with Elle.

Good thing Gabe had no intention of playing fair.

CHAPTER SEVEN

Apparently Elle hadn't outgrown her thing for bad ideas. And every time she thought things couldn't get any more complicated, she tumbled down another step and lost a bit more dignity.

Which would explain why she was in a filthy bar, desperately trying to win a game of pool against a man who obviously knew his way around a billiards table. She should just leave. Call a cab and go back to the gallery and her safe life. Walking through the front door of this bar had been a mistake in the first place. So why was she still here?

Elle pushed the thought away and leaned over the table, sighting down her cue stick. She took her shot, breaking the triangle of balls neatly. A solid ball tipped into the corner pocket.

Good. She preferred solids to stripes. It was a foolish superstition, but one Elle had never been able to shake despite her brother constantly laughing at her.

Moving around the table, she gave Gabe a pointed look. "You're in my way."

He tipped his beer back, and it was everything she could do not to watch the way his throat worked as he swallowed. No man's throat should be so sexy. His shirt shifted, a sliver of ink peeking out of the neckline. *Yum*.

Good lord, what was she thinking? Just because she still wanted him didn't mean she could get lulled into this whole thing. She *hadn't* been thinking, which was the problem. Elle botched her next shot, hitting the cue ball too hard and scratching. Damn it, she had to concentrate.

Gabe played billiards like a pro, pocketing a ball and lining up the next shot in one smooth move. He cocked an eyebrow broken by a thin scar. How hadn't she noticed that before? "I'm going to enjoy that kiss."

Warmth surged beneath her skin, and Elle had no doubt she was blushing. "In your dreams." Okay, that would have been a lot more convincing if she didn't sound so freaking breathy.

"You have no idea."

He didn't sound like he was joking. She took a deep breath and forced her mind to still. It didn't matter. Nothing mattered but the next shot. She'd win this game and get the heck out of here. Then she wouldn't have to deal with Gabe and his brutish ways.

Salvation came in the form of her phone ringing. Or that was what she thought until she recognized the twang of the ringtone. Her mother. God, it was like she could sense when Elle was getting into trouble. With a sigh, Elle held up a finger. "A moment."

Gabe shrugged. "Take all the time you need."

Nice of him, but no way did she plan on being on the phone longer than necessary. Elle started to head outside but changed her mind. She seriously didn't want to be alone out there in this neighborhood. Resigning herself to Gabe hearing the whole darn conversation, she answered. "Hello, Mom."

"What could you have possibly been doing that it took you so long to answer?"

That was her mother, always assuming the worst. It didn't help that in this case she was right. "I was just away from my desk. What did you need?"

"Can't I just call to talk to my darling daughter?"

Considering she never called "just to talk" Elle didn't buy that for a second. "Of course, Mom. How are you?" She caught herself before she leaned against the wall—God only knew what she'd pick up from the stained wood.

"I'd be a lot better if you'd agree to go out with Sammy."

Not this again. Elle rubbed a hand over her mouth. "You know how I feel about him." Sam Masterson Jr. was a lecherous little freak, and last time she'd been forced into dinner with him, he'd tried to stick his hand up her skirt. For some reason, though, her mom couldn't see anything but a potential son-in-law. It probably helped that Sam Masterson Sr. owned the largest car dealership in town.

She glanced over to find Gabe resting against the pool table, watching her. Of course he wasn't even pretending not to eavesdrop. He crossed his arms over his chest, his muscles bunching with the movement. And that ink. Lord help her, but Elle could barely resist the urge to run her fingers over it.

As if she could sense Elle's thoughts, her mother sighed, the sound perfectly calculated to instill guilt in her children. For some reason

Elle's brother never seemed affected, but she couldn't shake the need to make things right. She spun away from the distracting sight of Gabe and rushed to fill the silence before her mother asked about the decidedly barlike sounds in the background. "I already told you, I'm interested in someone else." Someone who certainly wasn't Gabe. Because she wasn't interested in him. At all. She'd wanted *Nathan*, even if there was no way anything would happen with him now—not with Gabe in the picture mucking things up—but she was desperate to avoid another encounter with Sam.

"Well, Elle, you'll forgive me if I have doubts about your taste. I swear, the only boy you've chosen to bring home was…less than impressive. And you certainly have turned up your nose at every man I've set you up with since."

Elle bit her lip, and tried to stay calm. "I've got to go, Mom, the phone's ringing. I'll talk to you later."

Another sigh. "If you insist."

"Good-bye." Elle hung up before her mom could come up with something else to harp about.

When she turned around, Gabe was watching her with an unidentifiable look on his face. "Family troubles?"

"I don't want to talk about it." Standing here with *this* man in this sad excuse for a bar only brought home the truth. Her mother was right. Elle had terrible taste in men, and Gabe would just be another black mark against her. "Take your turn."

"Sure thing." When his next turn hit at the wrong angle, he only grinned. "Have fun with that shot."

It wasn't an easy one. She was penned in on three sides by stripes, but Elle had been practicing banking. Leaning down, she froze when she caught Gabe staring down her shirt. "Stop it."

"Can't blame a man for looking when the view is so nice."

"Yes, actually, I can." *Ignore him, ignore him, ignore him.* She checked the angles and hit the ball, nearly cursing when it flew wide. That wouldn't have been the hardest shot she'd ever made. She should have managed it. *Would have* if Gabe wasn't running his mouth and she wasn't still frazzled by her mother's call.

Gabe walked around the table, passing close enough that his chest rubbed against her back. "Distracted, babe?" His breath brushed her ear, sending waves of tingles through her body.

Unforgivable thoughts crowded her brain, images of him pressing her against the pool table, kissing her, holding her close while she came undone in his arms.

She already knew how that ended with guys like him, though. With cheating, lies, and tears.

Screw this game—she was getting out of here now. Elle slid away, making a beeline for the rack where the cue sticks went.

"Where are you going?"

"I'm done playing. I need to get back to work." Her hand shook as she fitted the stick into its place. Curse him a thousand times over for bringing her to this dump and then trying to bully his way into a kiss. He was a Neanderthal and she wanted no part of his games. Elle turned around and nearly shrieked when she ran into Gabe. "What the hell?"

"Hell, babe? Careful there, that's almost a curse word."

She started to inch away, but there was nowhere to go—at least not without rubbing her entire body against his. No way in heck Elle was going *there*, not when her idiot nipples perked up at the very thought. She gritted her teeth. "Stop calling me that."

Gabe leaned in, kissably close, and grinned.

"Make me."

There was a part of her—a small, pathetic part—that wanted to close the distance and kiss him. The rest of her was spitting mad. "Get. Out. Of. My. Way."

"Or what? You'll curse at me again? You forfeited, which means I won. I want my kiss."

"Fat chance of that happening."

Gabe pressed a finger to the underside of her chin, tilting her face up. Elle commanded her body to move, to slap him, to run, to do something other than stare helplessly at his mouth and sway toward him. His lips weren't overly full, but they were perfectly shaped. The kind of mouth that brought to mind wicked, wicked thoughts—thoughts a woman like her had no business contemplating.

Elle forced herself to speak. "Please." The word came out soft, nearly begging. What was she begging for? For him to let her go? To pin her against the wall and ravish her? Even she wasn't sure.

His lips brushed against hers, sending shocks through her system. Had she convinced herself that her reaction before was a fluke? It couldn't be. Not when the barest brush of his mouth had her reeling. Before Elle could do something stupid like wrap her arms around him, Gabe shook his head as if throwing off a trance. He dropped his hand and took a step back, breaking contact. "Let's go."

"Go?" Why was she arguing this? She should be thrilled he was backing off.

Those dark eyes saw far too much. "You owe me a kiss, but I'm not taking it until you want it."

She already wanted it. A whole lot. Elle forced a harsh laugh. "As if that'll ever happen.

He leaned in again, so fast she flinched. "Keep up the attitude and you'll be lucky if I don't make you beg for it."

"I don't want you. I never will." But already she'd gotten close to proving him right. Too close. Elle propped her hands on her hips and tried to stir up some righteous indignation. "Can we just go?"

Exactly what she'd wanted in the first place, despite the disappointment simmering in her stomach. Elle followed him to the bar, earning some nasty looks from the women as Gabe leaned over and handed the guy his credit card.

"What are you doing?"

He didn't even spare her a glance. "Paying for lunch."

She started to demand for him to let her pay half, but gave it up for a lost cause. Why bother?

He wasn't going to listen anyway. So she waited silently while he paid, then trailed behind him like a lost puppy when he led the way back outside.

She blinked in the afternoon sunlight, wondering if she'd tumbled down the rabbit hole when she climbed the stairs to Nathan's loft on Saturday. This certainly felt more like Wonderland than her carefully planned reality. Which was wrong. So very, very wrong.

Everything in her life was balanced perfectly. It didn't have a place for freaky dive bars and men with so much testosterone she could barely breathe past it. Even though he and Nathan were similar looking, everything about Gabe still seemed too big, too male, too uncontrollable. He was the type of man who left a trail of women broken and weeping behind him—women like her. Elle wanted no part of it.

Forget the lost puppy act. She marched to the passenger door, getting there before he could open it for her, and slid into the seat. The leather stuck to her skin, adding to the claustrophobic feeling. She had to get out of here—away from this place that smelled like grease and stale beer and cigarette smoke—and back to her clean and orderly existence.

Gabe started the car and threw it into gear. They flew out of the parking lot and raced through the streets, breaking more than a few traffic laws in the process. Even though she'd promised herself she wouldn't talk to him anymore, Elle couldn't let this stand. "Slow down, please."

"What?" He blinked as if he'd been a thousand miles away. Fantastic. He was mentally wandering while risking her life and limb.

Maybe she should just keep her mouth shut, but… "You're going nearly fifteen miles over the speed limit."

"That's a problem for you, I take it. Christ, babe, don't you ever let your hair down? If you did, it'd probably help with the stick you have shoved up your ass."

Elle gaped at him. There's no way he'd just said that to her. What kind of man talked like that to his date? "Do you kiss your mother with that mouth?"

A shadow flickered in his dark eyes before he turned back to the road. "My mother's dead."

Damn it, she'd known that. Nathan didn't talk about his family much, but Ian had once mentioned that both his parents were deceased. Elle let her head fall back against the headrest and closed her eyes. "I'm sorry."

"Why? Not like you killed her."

Her eyes flew open and she glared at him. "Do you have to be so crass? You know what? Never mind. It doesn't matter—none of this matters."

Gabe shook his head and flipped on the radio, turning it up as death metal screeched through the speakers. He didn't want to talk anymore? Fine with her. Elle would be happy when this disaster of a date was over.

They roared through downtown, jerking to a stop across from the gallery's door. Elle shoved open the door as he reached for the volume, determined to get out before Gabe said something else to make her even angrier. She slammed the door and strode around the front bumper, barely resisting the urge to flip him off. It wasn't something she'd normally even consider, but this man seemed to bring out a part of her she'd never known existed.

He leaned out the window. "I'll see you around."

"Don't hold your breath." Elle crossed the street and pushed through the front door, feeling his gaze boring into her the entire time. It didn't matter. It was over and if she had her way, she was never going to see Gabe Schultz again.

CHAPTER EIGHT

Five whole days passed while Gabe argued with himself about Elle. Five days of flip-flopping and bitching to Nathan about her. She thought he was trash, thought he wasn't fit to kiss her disgustingly perfect feet. Gabe didn't need to spend time chasing a chick like that. There were plenty of women in town who would be more than happy to jump into bed with him, let alone gain a more permanent position.

"I don't understand women." He swept the tattoo gun over Paul's arm, shading in the pair of wolves.

"You and me both, brother." Paul was one of his regulars, and Gabe always made time for him when he was in town. It didn't matter how long the waiting list was, Paul got one of the top spots if he wanted it.

"I thought you had that redhead," Gabe said. "What's her name? Laney?"

"Lee. Yeah, it's over. Has been for a while."

Well shit. Gabe kept shading, darkening the corners and fading them out to blend in with the top of where Paul's sleeve would start—once he figured out what he wanted. "I'm sorry."

"No reason to be. So who's the broad that's got you all tangled up in knots?"

He didn't want to talk about Elle, even if she was all he thought about during his downtime. "Just some chick."

"Bullshit."

"She's a good girl—not the type who's comfortable with all this." He waved to the tattoo shop. It was more home to him than any house he owned, Gabe's personality etched through every inch of it, from the movie posters on the walls to the red and black coloring. Even more than his nightclubs, this shop was *his*.

Picturing the horror on Elle's face if she ever mistakenly walked through the door made him frown. Then again, maybe she wouldn't freak out. She seemed to appreciate good ink when she saw it, unlike so many other women who gushed over the fact that he had tattoos without bothering to ask about the stories behind them. Didn't matter, though. "She's not for me."

"As if that's ever stopped you."

Gabe snorted. "That's what Nathan said. I think you guys are confusing me with someone who chases women. I don't have time for that shit." He thought back, wondering when was the last time he'd actually been interested enough to try. Six months? A year? Too long. Which had to be the reason he was borderline obsessed with Elle. Maybe he just needed some stranger to wash away the memory of her in his arms.

"I'm not talking women, though maybe the reason you've never chased one down before is because you never found one worth chasing."

"Thanks for that, Yoda." Gabe dragged the needles over Paul's arm a little harder than necessary, but the big man didn't so much as flinch. "This one's different. A country corn princess of all things. I don't know what to do with her. Either way, it doesn't matter—she's not into me."

"Then you haven't tried hard enough."

The problem was, Gabe didn't know how to go about any of this. It wasn't something he liked admitting but, damn it, he needed help. "I don't even know where to start."

"Flowers, man. Chicks dig flowers."

Flowers, huh? He sat back and looked at the tat. Pretty damn good, if he did say so himself. "You're done. Check it out."

After Paul gave his approval, Gabe bandaged it up and waved away the cash. "No charge this time. You helped me out."

Paul shook his head. "I just told you what any shitty rom-com would. Go watch *The Notebook* or something. Apparently that's the standard women are putting to relationships now. A real guy can hardly compete."

"Now who's talking bullshit?"

"I know, right?" Paul grabbed his leather jacket and headed for the door. "See you."

Gabe set about disposing of his needles and cleaning up his work space, but his mind wasn't in it. Did he really want to pursue this? Elle wasn't just gorgeous, she was a lady. A stuck-up one, but a lady nonetheless. Women like that expected certain stuff he didn't know the first thing about. Maybe Paul was right, and he should just buy her some flowers.

Gabe picked up his phone and dialed Nathan. "Hey, meet me at that grocery store by your house."

"Hello to you, too."

"Yeah, yeah. Hi. I'll see you in twenty." He hung up before Nathan could say no.

Gabe closed up the shop and then headed north. His brother had a house on the very edges of Spokane, close enough for easy access to all the necessities, but tucked away in a copse of trees that afforded it some much-valued privacy. Personally, Gabe was of the mind that if you were going to live in the country, you should goddamn well live in the country—which is why his house was well beyond the city limits. The only problem was its location made it a pain in the ass to get into town.

So he crashed at Nathan's house more often than not—a fact his brother constantly ribbed him over. Hell, he'd threatened to start charging Gabe rent.

But there was another reason Gabe only went up to the house every so often, one he'd never admit to his brother even though he was pretty sure Nathan felt the same way. It was so freaking lonely to come home to an empty place. He couldn't even have a dog because he was out of town so often. All that greeted him when he walked through the door was a cold, impenetrable silence.

He turned up the radio, letting the music

roll through him. There was no reason to go all emo over it. He didn't like being alone. So sue him. There was nothing wrong with that. For some reason, though, being around Elle and all the challenges she represented only made the loneliness worse. She didn't think they were compatible.

Well, Gabe was going to prove her wrong.

Despite the traffic, he got there at the same time as his brother, pulling up next to the jacked-up black Ford F-150. As he climbed out of the Camaro, Nathan hopped down. "You want to tell me what's going on?"

"We're going to buy some flowers." It sounded really stupid when he said it aloud. Gabe ignored his brother's smirk. "And I need you to tell me everything you know about Elle."

"Elle? I thought you'd decided to let that go."

He thought he had too. "I'm not done yet."

"She's been stomping around the gallery all week, with steam practically shooting out her ears." Nathan crossed his arms over his chest. "I suppose this is going to make it worse?"

"Probably."

"Good to know."

They headed into the grocery store, veering left off the door and into the flower section.

Gabe turned a full circle, taking in the rainbow of colors. "Holy shit. How is someone supposed to pick from this?"

"You could just buy her roses."

"Roses are lame."

Nathan tapped two fingers to his chin. "Hmm. I seem to remember Elle saying something similar a few months ago."

"You're not helping." Gabe pulled off one of the plastic bag things used to make a bouquet. "What's her favorite color?"

"Purple. Or maybe pink."

Gabe shot him a look. "Hasn't she worked for you for damn near a year?"

"Well, yeah."

"And you don't even know her favorite color?" Maybe bringing Nathan along hadn't been the best idea. At this rate, his brother was just as likely to steer him down the wrong road as the right one.

Nathan shrugged. "It's never come up. But she wears a lot of those, so it stands to reason."

"Fair enough." Gabe started grabbing random purple and pink flowers, trying to get a good variety. Chicks liked variety, right? "What else can you tell me?"

"She's girly. I'm pretty sure the woman

would drop dead at the idea of camping. Like I said before, I served with her brother. He didn't talk about his family a lot, but his little sister was untouchable in his mind. I know their parents are still alive and still married, but that's about it."

Of course they were. It was exactly the type of family unit Gabe could picture around her. They were probably just as goody-goody as Elle was. Then again, there had been definite tension on her face during her phone call with her mom. Trouble on the home front? It was something to think about. "What else?"

"God, you don't ask for much, do you? It's not like we sit around, braiding each other's hair and gossiping." Nathan picked some tall flowers and shoved them into the bouquet. "She's an amazing coordinator—has a great eye for art and a passion to go with it. I've never met anyone who can identify so perfectly with what the artist is trying to get across."

There was something like wonder in his brother's voice. Gabe stopped short. "Are you sure you're not into her? Because you sure as hell sound like you are."

"It's not like that. I enjoy her company and we can spend hours talking about art but…" Nathan looked away for a second and when he turned back, he was his usual easygoing self. "Enough about me. Let's get this paid for and help you get the girl."

Gabe let it go because he had his suspicions about where that shadow had come from. Some things you couldn't talk about, even with family. *Especially* with family. Nathan had proved that time and again when it came to that mystery girl he dated ages ago. "Let's do it."

It was only when they were in the checkout line that reality set in. It was Friday night—even someone as uptight as Elle wasn't likely to be home by herself. What if she had a date? Oh, he didn't like the thought of that at all. "This is a shitty idea."

Nathan flipped through one of the trashy celebrity magazines. "What's wrong now? I swear you're PMS-ing or something."

"Not funny."

"Yes, well, I'm not a comedian. Speak, so we can pay for the damn flowers."

"It's Friday night. I have no idea where she is." Even if she was home alone, it would be seriously creepy if he showed up uninvited.

"Oh, that." Nathan tossed the magazine onto the grocery line. "She's with her friend Roxanne at Twigs—the north one, if I'm not mistaken."

"I thought you didn't know a goddamn thing about her." Gabe swiped his credit card.

"We don't have deep, heartfelt conversations, but she's a woman. Women talk."

Thank God they did, or he'd be sitting at home by himself, staring at a bouquet of flowers that only served to remind him Elle wasn't interested. He gathered them up and headed for the parking lot.

Nathan laughed and climbed into his truck. "You're just going to walk in there and hand her the flowers, aren't you?"

Well, yeah, that had been the plan. Gabe paused. "Do you have a better idea?"

"Nope. Just kind of wish I was there to watch it all go down." His diesel engine roared to life. "Good luck."

As Gabe watched his little brother drive away, he was pretty damn sure he was going to need all the luck he could get.

CHAPTER NINE

Elle swirled a straw through her martini and wondered if she should just take it as a shot. "I really don't want to talk about it."

"Yes, you really do." Roxanne whipped out a compact and checked her lipstick. It was perfect, just like always, but that didn't stop her from being OCD about it. Considering the brilliant red she preferred, Elle didn't blame her paranoia.

Desperate to talk about anything other than her failed seduction and crappy date, she nodded at the bartender. He grinned and waltzed over to them, the very picture of tall, dark, and handsome. "Ladies. How're the drinks coming?"

"I think we're ready for another. I'm Elle, by the way. This is my friend Roxanne." Elle downed her drink in a single gulp as the two eyed each other. Though her friend claimed she was too busy with work to date, it didn't stop Roxanne from surveying the possibilities. Even if she never took advantage of them.

Sure enough, when he went back to fill their order, the brunette leaned in. "If that man isn't sex on a stick, I don't know who is. If I had the time…"

"Why don't you?"

Roxanne held up a finger. "I know what you're trying to do and it won't work. Stop stalling and spill the details. Remember"—she pointed at herself—"living vicariously through your deviant sexual exploits."

"You make me sound like I'm slutting around town."

"Some days I wish you were. Think of the stories. Oh, don't look at me like that. You know I'm only joking." When it became apparent Elle wasn't going to respond, she sighed. "Let's start with something easy. How'd the date go?"

This, at least, she could talk about without blushing and stammering. "Terrible. He took me to a freaking dive bar. Thank God I didn't have to use the bathroom or I would have walked away with syphilis. As it is, I'm pretty sure I picked up hepatitis."

"Did you make a doctor's appointment to check it out?"

Elle started to admit that she had before she realized Roxanne was only poking fun. Maybe she was being a bit overdramatic, but she couldn't be too careful—especially since she had an orgasm with a total stranger. A really intense, really mind-blowing orgasm. Pushing that away, she focused on the story. "Well, after I eat the questionable food, he decides we're going to play pool. Then, my freaking mom called."

Roxanne made a choking sound. "That harpy has terrifying timing."

"She's my *mother*."

"That doesn't make her any less a harpy." She motioned. "What happened after that delightful conversation?"

Delightful was the last word she'd have used to describe it. "Not only are we playing pool in one of the grossest buildings I've ever been in, but there has to be a bet involved too."

"A bet." Roxanne's green eyes practically lit up. "Oh, do tell."

Okay, so maybe this story wasn't all that much easier to tell than the sex one. Elle looked for a napkin to shred, but there were only the heavy-duty coasters. "He wanted a kiss."

"Oh. My. God."

Elle jumped, feeling guilty for no reason at all. "What?"

"You wanted him to kiss you."

"I did not!"

"Yes you did, you little hussy." Roxanne grinned. "I don't judge."

She bit her lip, temporarily saved when the bartender brought their drinks back. As soon as he was gone, however, there was no denying it. "Okay, yes. Maybe a little. You have to understand, he's so wrong for me. Like the exact opposite of what I should want in a husband or boyfriend or whatever. But…"

Elle took a hasty drink and nearly choked. This was way stronger than the last one. Maybe it was alcohol loosening her tongue, or maybe she just needed to get it out in the air, but she didn't stop there. "I don't know, Rox. There's something really, really attractive about him in a Neanderthal sort of way. Like you look at him and want to have him haul you back to his cave, and have his wicked way with you."

Holy crap, she couldn't believe she'd just admitted that out loud. But it felt kind of good to say it so Elle kept going, toying with her straw as she went on. "I mean, sure he's rough around the edges, but his tattoos are amazing and that mouth is just *sinful*."

"Yes…yes it is."

She frowned at the weird look on her friend's face. "Rox?" Then she realized Roxanne wasn't looking at her.

She was focusing on some point over Elle's shoulder.

The room swayed as all the blood rushed from her head and foreboding slammed through her system. This couldn't be happening. There was seriously no way this was happening. "Please tell me he's not standing right behind me."

Roxanne put her elbows on the table and propped her chin in her hands as if getting ready to watch a show. "He's totally right behind you."

Elle turned, feeling as if she were swimming through molasses. Sure enough, Gabe stood not two feet from her, holding…flowers? From the grin on his face, he'd heard every single word. She waited for lightning to strike her dead, but apparently God wasn't in an obliging mood tonight.

When he held out the flowers, she took them with numb hands. She lifted the flowers and inhaled on reflex, still unable to tear her gaze from Gabe. Tonight he wore a basic black T-shirt, but it clung to every single freaking muscle. The jeans did the same darn thing. It wasn't fair—not by a long shot.

Elle definitely needed another drink.

"So, you think my mouth is sinful?"

Good God, he really had been close enough to hear everything. "No." Behind her, Roxanne sounded like she was choking on her drink. Good. She deserved it for not warning Elle he was here and close enough to eavesdrop. "Your lips are way too thin, practically nonexistent."

Gabe took a step forward and leaned on the back of her chair, nearly overwhelming her with his closeness. "Oh, really?"

"Yes." Elle coughed, belatedly realizing her throat was kind of itchy.

"Because I'm pretty sure you just said my mouth is *sinful*."

This was so not okay. She rubbed her nose. "You misheard."

"I don't think I did." He leaned sideways around her. "You're Roxanne, right? I'm Gabe."

The traitor smiled sweetly at him and offered her hand. "Hello, Gabe. I've been hearing so much about you lately."

"*Rox.*"

"What? I'm only speaking the truth."

Gabe was having far too much fun with this. "You heard her call my mouth sinful, didn't you?"

"Don't you dare answer that, Roxanne." Elle sneezed. What the heck? She tilted the bouquet and groaned. "You bought me sage."

"I bought you what?"

"Sage." It was as if, by noticing it, her symptoms suddenly became ten times worse. Elle's eyes started watering and, if the itchiness of her arms were any indication, she was in the process of breaking out in hives. Awesome. Just freaking fantastic. She tossed the bouquet at Roxanne. "This isn't funny."

The brunette failed miserably in her attempt to stop laughing. "I'm sorry. It really isn't. This is horrible. But, holy crap, it's so terrible it's hilarious."

Elle rubbed her nose with the back of her hand, which, of course, only made the itching worse because the damned sage was all over her. "I hate you."

"No, you don't. You love me." Roxanne finished off her drink.

Gabe finally moved from around her chair to stand next to the table. From the way his eyes bugged out, the blotchiness had reached her face.

"What's happening?"

"Elle is allergic to sage." Oh great, *now* Roxanne could be helpful. "She blows up like a blimp whenever it gets within six feet of her, and you just handed her a bouquet full of the stuff."

"Holy shit. I'm so sorry. I just—"

"It's not a big deal." Elle scooted off the chair and grabbed her purse. "And to you, Roxanne, I only have one word: karma."

Elle marched out of the restaurant, trying not to notice the stares and whispers as she passed. She failed, just like she failed not to notice the heavy footsteps following her out. "Leave me alone."

"This is my fault. You gotta let me make this right." He jogged up until they were even, but was forced to fall back when Elle wove through the cars, heading for her Prius. "Please, Elle. I'm really sorry."

Considering her eyes were starting to swell, it probably wasn't the best idea to drive. Being safety-conscious was the only reason she said, "Fine. Whatever. I need allergy medication. Fast."

"Fast I can do, babe." He hooked an arm around her waist and steered her toward his red monstrosity.

Elle slid into the passenger seat and closed

her eyes, focusing on breathing. All she wanted right now was a tub of Benadryl, a shower, and a bag of frozen peas for her face. And sleep—a whole lot of sleep. It would be okay. A quick stop at the store and she'd be home free. She could do this.

The car swerved so violently, Elle was thrown back in her seat. "Hey, watch it!"

"You said fast."

She had, but she didn't want him to kill her in the process. "I'm not going to die—I just need some allergy meds."

"Die? Is that even possible from *flowers*?"

"Yes." She clutched the seat as he swerved again. "You keep driving like this and I'm going to vomit all over your leather seats."

"Small price to pay if I can help you be less miserable faster. It'll be okay. We're almost there."

Thank God, because she didn't think she could deal with this much longer. His concern might have been endearing under different circumstances, but Elle was about ready to freak out and start scratching every part of her body she could reach. Compared with that kind of annoyance, Gabe just needed to shut the hell up and get her some Benadryl.

Chapter Ten

Gabe was a goddamn idiot. He'd never stopped to consider Elle might be allergic to something. Though, seriously, who could have guessed she was allergic to *sage*, or that the grocery store would even stock something like that in the flower section?

He cut through traffic, taking the opportunity to check on her. Holy shit. Angry red blotches covered her pale skin, clearly visible even in the fading evening light. Though he couldn't be sure, he thought maybe the skin around her eyes was swelling too. He tightened his grip on the steering wheel, determined to fix the mess he'd made.

An old yellow Volkswagen cut him off and slowed down, until they were crawling up to the blatantly green light. He muttered under his breath, riding their ass. They needed to get the hell out of the way before Gabe *made* them get out of the way.

"You know, I'd feel a lot better about this if I was sure we weren't going to end up in a fiery ball of death."

"Yeah, well, that won't matter if your throat starts swelling and you die in my passenger seat." That could happen with an allergic reaction. He'd seen it on the Discovery Channel.

Elle choked out a laugh. "I'm just miserable, not dying."

She might be thinking that now, but it was possible that the full reaction hadn't hit. Things would keep getting worse until they got the meds into her system. With another curse, he flipped on his turn signal and cut across two lanes, earning a startled curse from Elle. They veered into the lot and skidded to a stop in the parking spot closest to the doors.

"This is a handicapped parking spot."

"So I'll get a ticket." Gabe threw open his door and ran around the front of the car to get hers. "Let me help you."

"I'm fine." Elle shoved past him and marched toward the store. "You're acting insane."

"And you didn't look for cars. What if you got

hit?" Christ, he sounded like a mother hen.

Apparently Elle thought the same thing. "Thanks, Mom, but I'm a grown-up. I have no intention of throwing myself in front of a car." She hurried inside, but Gabe could have sworn he heard her mutter, "But I might if you don't stop nagging me."

Gabe searched for the medicine aisle, but apparently Elle knew her way around because she was already there by the time he figured out where it was. She grabbed the generic brand, but he snatched it out of her hand. "Get Benadryl."

"It's the same thing."

"No, it's not." When she didn't move fast enough, he reached around her and put the box back. The name brand was two bucks more, but it was a small price to pay when Elle's health was on the line. "Take some now."

Elle jerked away as if he'd waved a dead animal in her face. "I'm not opening this box and taking medicine right here in the aisle. That's against the rules."

Gabe glared. "You already know how this goes. Take the damn meds or I'm going to force it down your throat."

"You really know how to show a woman a good time." But instead of flipping him the bird, she watched him open the box and dole out a dose of the gross pink liquid. Elle took it as a shot. "We done yet?"

Not by a long shot. "No. We need…" He shoved the stuff back into the box, and considered. What else would she need? God, he didn't know the first thing about this crap. That stupid show on the Discovery Channel had focused more on the dying part and less on the treating it.

"While you're figuring that out, I'll be walking this way."

He followed her, eyeing the contents of each aisle they passed. Chocolates—chocolates would be good. Chicks dug that stuff when they weren't feeling good. Gabe veered into that aisle and started to choose some random brands. Then he stopped. What if she was allergic to nuts or something?

Carefully examining the nutritional facts on the back of each package, he decided on basic milk chocolate and dark chocolate. On second thought, maybe he should get some of the white stuff too. There was no telling what Elle would like, but she'd already proven she was particular about weird things.

He walked in the general direction she'd

gone, but stopped in front of the soup section. Did an allergic reaction count as sick? Maybe he should pick up some chicken noodle soup too... Yeah, good idea. The Campbell's kind was what he used to give Nathan when they were kids. Before he could second-guess himself, Gabe added two cans to the stuff in his arms.

On a whim, he stopped in the bath and body section and picked a few different bubble bath bottles. He wasn't a fan of the whole bath thing, but Elle seemed like she'd be into it, and he remembered something about taking baths when you have chicken pox. Maybe it was the same for allergic reactions.

A cart would have been a good idea, but it was too late now. He shifted the stuff until nothing was in danger of falling and kept going, glancing down each aisle as he passed. Elle was nowhere to be seen.

She wouldn't have left without him, right?

Hell, of course she would.

Gabe spun around, ready to drop everything and go sprinting after her. Then he caught a glimpse of her on the other side of the store. She had something pressed against her face—he recognized it as frozen peas when he got closer.

"There you are."

"Here I am." She sighed and lifted the bag long enough to frown. "What's all that?"

"Ah…" He felt stupid standing in front of her, his arms overflowing with random crap. Maybe he should have just left everything alone and gone with her to the freezer section. "I thought you might want some of this."

Elle leaned in, nearly smacking him in the face with her frozen peas. "Chocolate, bubble bath, and chicken noodle soup."

"I didn't know what would help, so I got a bit of everything."

"I…see." Those blue eyes focused on him, and Gabe suddenly felt like he had when, at ten, he'd hung Joey Pandini's dirty underwear from the flagpole, and had to sit two hours outside the principal's office waiting to see if his mom would show up.

She hadn't.

Elle finally broke the moment by shoving the peas back against her face. "Can we go, please?"

"Yeah, sure. My bad." Gabe dumped everything into the cashier's lane and tapped his foot as the teenager rang everything up. The kid moved so slow, Gabe was tempted to toss him aside and do it himself.

"I need the peas, ma'am."

With a long-suffering sigh, Elle handed them over. He wasn't sure, but Gabe thought her skin was a little less red. Either that or it looked less red because red covered every inch he could see. It was hard to tell in this light. "We should go to the hospital." Why hadn't he thought of that first? It was the logical thing to do.

She accepted the peas back from the kid. "We're not going to the hospital."

"You could go into anaphylactic shock—"

"Gabe. Stop." She actually reached out and put her hand on his arm. Every muscle in his body jumped to attention, which was damned inconvenient at the moment. For her part, Elle didn't seem to notice his pants fitting him a bit tighter. "I'm really going to be okay."

"Are you sure? Because it's no trouble to get you there." He mentally mapped the route—ten minutes, tops. Sure, they might break a few traffic laws along the way, but what was that compared to Elle's safety?

"I'm fine. Promise." She held out her pinkie. When Gabe just stared, Elle reached down and hooked his pinkie with hers, giving it a firm shake. "See. We're good."

Who the hell pinkie swore after grade school? He wasn't even sure he'd done it *in* grade school. Shaking his head, he paid for their stuff and walked with her back to the car. It wasn't until they were both inside, the motor running, that he realized he had no idea where she lived. "Where am I headed?"

She flipped down the visor and checked her face in the mirror. "I think the swelling's going down—you can just drop me at my car."

"Yeah, right."

"You're seriously not going to let this go, are you?"

"Are you surprised?"

Elle draped the peas back over her face and sighed. "No. Take 395 North. Hatch exit. First right and then another right. Third house on the left."

It seemed easy enough. Gabe exited the parking lot and drove north. Night had fallen completely while they were inside, and there was something relaxing about leaving the city limits. For half a second he considered continuing on the highway and going to his house, but he nixed the idea—Elle would be most comfortable in her own home.

Following her directions, he found himself in one of the many suburbs that were scattered at the northernmost edge of Spokane. At least in this one the houses weren't crammed together, each sporting a decent front yard—and backyard, if the size of the fences were any indication. His headlights coasted over Elle's house as he pulled into the driveway, revealing it to be a cheery yellow. There was even a hanging pot of flowers on the porch.

Somehow, Gabe wasn't surprised. He put the Camaro in park and wondered what his life would have been like if he grew up in a house like this. Different. Really different. It was the kind of life he wanted for the future, for the kids he'd recently decided were part of the plan. Christ, but he was so tired of the aching loneliness that was eating him alive.

CHAPTER ELEVEN

Having Gabe in her home felt…odd. Elle rolled her shoulders, trying to scratch without actually scratching. What she needed was a shower, but she didn't particularly want to leave him wandering around her house, taking up too much space. She scratched the inside of her elbow and froze when he focused on the move. "You aren't better."

"It takes a while for the Benadryl to kick in." But the reaction wouldn't stop for good until she had this crap off her skin. "You want to watch some television while I jump in the shower really quick?"

His gaze skated over her, so intense it was as if he'd run his hand down the front of her body. Okay, wow. Maybe she needed to take a cold shower. Like, now.

"Living room is that way." She waved at the doorway behind him and backed toward the stairs. "I'll only be a minute."

Gabe shadowed her retreat. "You shouldn't be alone right now."

Oh lordy. "I'm not alone. You're here." She motioned at the front room as she started up the stairs. "I mean, not *here*-here, but in the same house. If my throat starts closing, I promise to scream for help."

"If your throat starts closing, you won't be able to scream for anything."

His words shouldn't make her think of sex. They really shouldn't. But, seriously, could anyone blame her? Here he was, stalking her up the stairs toward her room, and she couldn't help but remember the last time they'd been in a bedroom together.

No. Bad idea. Really bad idea.

"Stop." She held up a hand.

He didn't stop walking until her hand rested against the middle of his chest. With her standing a stair above him, they were almost the same height. "I don't need to be in the shower with you, but I'm not leaving you alone until you're past this reaction."

"You're being paranoid." Her voice came out breathy and low. Crap. Elle made an effort to sound normal. "And where, exactly, do you plan on waiting?"

Gabe grinned, the wolfish expression making the breath stall in her lungs. "The bathroom, of course."

"Of course…"

She wasn't sure how he did it, but the next thing she knew, she was sitting on the bathroom counter and Gabe was taking off her heels. "I really like these, by the way."

"Oh." Elle watched him unhook the second shoe, carefully sliding it off her foot. She could just imagine how he'd stand and pull off her shirt, then move on to each article of clothing until she was naked, all while using the same gentle touches. She shivered, trying vainly to keep her toes from curling.

"Are you okay? You aren't having a seizure, are you?"

For a second she thought he was teasing her, but there was nothing except concern in his dark gaze. She pushed to her feet before she convinced herself that his stripping her was a fantastic idea. "I…" Her words trailed off at the look on his face, eyes gone nearly black with something like need.

Elle found herself holding her breath, waiting to see what he'd do. Would he insist on continuing to help her? God, what if he took her right here on the bathroom counter? She bit her lip, another shiver racking her body.

"Are you cold?" There was no mistaking the fact that Gabe knew exactly what the source of her shiver was. He braced his hands on her hips, his chest brushing against hers. "Elle, I asked you a question."

He had, hadn't he? "No, I'm not cold."

"You need to get into the shower."

"Yes, I do."

His hands coasted up over her sides, taking her shirt off in a smooth move. As he tossed it to the side, Elle tried to come up with a protest. But what was there to protest? She wanted him to touch her more than she wanted her next breath. Gabe didn't keep her waiting, tracing a single finger over the pink lace of her bra. "I like this better than your shoes."

What was she supposed to say to that? "Thank you."

Gabe moved back down to her skirt, undoing it carefully, the draw of the zipper unnaturally loud in the bathroom. Was she really going to do this? It was undoubtedly a mistake. A really big one. But, with her body practically quivering with need, Elle suddenly didn't care.

He went to his knees and helped her step out of her skirt. Then Gabe sat back on his heels and just *looked* at her. "Christ, you're beautiful."

It didn't mean anything. Words were less than worthless—easy to throw out there, even easier to take back. Oh, but how she wanted him to mean them, though. Elle bit her lip, waiting to see what he'd do next.

Finally, Gabe reached down and covered her hand with his own. Elle blinked. She'd been scratching without even realizing she was doing it. He brought her hand to his lips and pressed a kiss against her knuckles. "You need to get this stuff off your skin."

"You're right." She took a step back and her knees buckled. Gabe caught her easily before she fell. The heat of his hands on her bare skin felt so good. Too good. She didn't want it to stop. Which meant she really needed it to stop. Elle steadied herself on his shoulders. "Jeesh. I don't know what's wrong with me."

"You're having an allergic reaction and are doped up on meds. It's understandable." He stood and, keeping an arm around her waist, leaned into the shower to turn it on.

"What are you doing?" Elle watched, wide-eyed, as he took off his shirt. Whoa, those were some serious muscles. And, sure, she'd felt them the night they were together and had started painting them—not that she'd ever admit *that*—but they were so much more *real* now.

Not to mention all the tattoos. She couldn't tear her gaze from the odd mechanical one taking up half his chest and arm. Gears and pulleys, it looked like. The bottom part of it traced the top of his abs, drawing her attention south. Good God, his body was overwhelming. She wanted to lick the edge of that tattoo, explore its intricacies with her mouth.

His hands went to his pants and her jaw dropped. "Gabe…"

"Relax." He shot her a surprisingly playful grin. "I'm not going to take advantage of you in your moment of weakness. But I don't want you collapsing and hurting yourself."

She should probably argue, but then his pants were off and Elle couldn't focus on anything but his thighs. Wow. Just…wow. The black boxer-briefs molded to his body perfectly, leaving little to the imagination, and she couldn't help but notice how turned on he was. Gabe turned to test the temperature of the water and she actually whimpered at the sight of his butt.

"Is something wrong?"

Yes. No. Maybe? All Elle knew was that her ability to resist touching him was fading fast. She sneezed.

"Come on, babe. Let's get you cleaned off." He yanked back the curtain enough to step in and pull her in after him. Immediately, Gabe moved aside and shifted her under the water. It couldn't have been all that warm for him with the one showerhead, but he didn't seem to mind. Instead, he nodded at her shower caddy. "Soap?"

Elle handed him her body wash and tried really hard not to notice how the water had plastered his already-tight underwear to his skin. God, the man was temptation personified. For his part, he seemed all for keeping his word to not take advantage of her. While she was trying to decide if that was a good thing or a bad thing, Gabe soaped up his hands. "Arms."

He moved from one to the other, his big hands sliding over her skin. First her arms, then shoulders, bypassing her breasts to her stomach. Each touch had the heat at her core winding tighter until she was almost panting with need. Then he was on his knees in front of her. Again.

Elle bit her lip as she watched him, his brow furrowed in concentration, as if washing her were the most important thing in the world.

Once her legs were clean enough for his satisfaction, Gabe paused, hands on the outside of her thighs. Guess he'd finally noticed the fact the water had made her panties and bra darn near transparent. She could almost feel the stroke of his stare as he moved forward until his breath ghosted over her skin.

Would he kiss her there? Did she want him to? God, this had nothing to do with want. She needed him. Elle was already wound so tightly, she was half convinced that a single touch would send her spiraling over the edge.

But Gabe didn't touch her.

He blew out a breath and pushed to his feet. "You should be good now."

Good? There was nothing good about this.

Except…

He'd kept his word. Even when it had to be painfully obvious of how much she wanted him to break it. Elle moved so he could turn off the water and then accepted the towel he offered. When he pointedly looked the other way, she stepped out of the tub.

Gabe cleared his throat. "I'm going to take a

shower."

"Yes, okay." She nodded, eager to put some distance between them before she did something unbearably stupid, like throwing herself into his arms and begging him to make her come again. "Let me see if I can find something that will fit you." Hopefully the task would keep her distracted long enough to calm down her hormones. Elle was pretty sure she had a pair of Ian's sweats stashed somewhere in the back of her closet. She headed for her closet, trying to ignore the devastatingly sexy half-naked man in her bathroom.

God help her.

CHAPTER TWELVE

Gabe was *not* going to masturbate in her shower. He leaned into the spray and turned the water colder, hoping it would kill his raging erection. The way Elle had eye-fucked him while he soaped up her body really hadn't helped with his control. As it stood, he was hanging by a thread. He waited until he couldn't stand the freezing temperature before he turned off the water and stepped out of the shower.

He had almost thrown caution to the wind and ripped off Elle's panties. Really, who would have blamed him? She'd been so close, her body shaking beneath his touch, everything he wanted right there in his face, practically begging for his mouth. If he'd licked his way down her stomach, she wouldn't have stopped him. No, if her response was anything to go by, she might just have urged him on.

But he'd promised he wouldn't take advantage of her, and it had become vitally important to him that he keep his word to this woman.

Gabe grabbed a fluffy pink towel off the rack and cursed himself. He was a grown-ass man—he could be in the same room with Elle without tossing her onto her back and banging her brains out. At least he could as long as she kept those control-unraveling looks to herself.

He opened the door slowly, wanting to give her plenty of time to hear him coming. "Elle?"

"In here."

Following the sound of her voice across the bedroom, Gabe peeked into a walk-in closet. The damn thing was filled to the brim with all sorts of chick crap, but somewhere along the way she'd found a pair of raggedy sweats and was holding them up proudly. But he had eyes only for her. She wore a tiny pair of pink shorts with a drawstring that just begged for him to undo.

Damn it, he needed to focus on something else.

Gabe dragged his gaze up, but he never made it to her face. The white tank top was borderline see-through and he couldn't help but notice she wasn't wearing a bra. Why the hell wasn't she wearing a bra? Hadn't the shower been enough of a test—one he'd passed with flying colors, thank you very much? This woman was obviously trying to kill him.

With a Herculean effort, he focused above her shoulders. She'd pulled her hair into a high ponytail. Between that and her fresh-scrubbed face, Elle was the very picture of the girl next door. More like the wet dream next door.

"Um...you're staring."

He couldn't help it, nor could he help noticing she seemed to like his eyes on her body. Gabe cursed as he grabbed the sweatpants out of her hands and hurried back to the bathroom. It was rude, but the peace between them was too fragile to ruin because his dick was making a tent of the stupid pink towel. He took his time dressing, helped along by the fact the sweats were too small. Old and gray, they obviously weren't hers.

So whose were they? An ex-boyfriend's, maybe kept for their nostalgic memories? Yeah, he didn't like that idea. He kind of wanted to wear them home and then have a bonfire in his backyard—not the most well adjusted plan, but he liked it.

By the time he'd dressed, he had his physical reaction under control. Still, it was going to be a long-ass night with her prancing around in those cute little booty shorts. Before he could make it back into the bedroom, a faint ringing came from the pile of his clothes on the bathroom floor. Who the hell was calling him right now? Not Nathan, that was for damn sure. Gabe fished his phone out of the clothes on the floor. "Hello?"

"We have a problem."

He sighed and rubbed the bridge of his nose. "Lynn." If the new G.M. of the L.A. club was calling him, it'd have to be a big problem. She wasn't the type to need hand-holding. "What's going on?"

"Like I said, we have a problem. That douche you fired? He's threatening a lawsuit if he's not compensated."

Christ, this was the last thing he needed. "He was skimming off the top. What judge is going to rule in his favor?"

"Don't know and don't care. He wants to talk to you personally."

"He's got my number."

"Yeah, well, he wants a face-to-face meeting to discuss things."

Gabe watched Elle stack some folded blankets on her bed. He shut the door and lowered his voice. "I'm not flying down there like some fucking dog he's called to heel without talking to him first. Give him my number if he doesn't have it already."

"I thought you might say that." She sighed. "I'll see what I can do."

"Thanks, Lynn."

"You can thank me with a raise, sweet cheeks."

He laughed. "You keep this thing running smoothly and it's yours."

"I'll remember you said that."

He hung up and walked back into the bedroom. Elle gave an oddly shaky smile. "Problem?"

"Just some work stuff." Stuff he didn't want to think about with her standing there, looking so adorably sexy. "You have any movies?"

She blinked. "Uh, yeah."

Duh. Of course she had movies. Everyone had movies these days. Christ, the longer he was around her, the stupider he sounded. Gabe cleared his throat. "Might as well watch one. I don't think either of us is getting much sleep tonight. And you need another dose of meds."

Elle rolled her eyes, but she didn't bother to argue. He followed her down the stairs, taking the time to examine his surroundings—and keep his eyes off her ass. The pale carpet and paint should have created a washed-out vibe, but instead they seemed to be created solely to frame the bright prints lining the walls. Gabe recognized several different local artists he'd seen in Nathan's gallery, people who did everything from portraits to landscapes to abstract. Somehow she'd managed to meld them together so they didn't appear chaotic. He approved.

The kitchen was painted a crisp lime green that offset white cabinets and appliances, and everything was immaculate. Either she never used it or she was a complete neat freak. "You cook?"

She stopped in the doorway and shrugged. "Not really. I manage to screw up boiling water. Makes my mom despair at my ability to ever find a husband."

At least there was something she couldn't do. The woman was enough to give any man a complex. Gabe wandered around the island and opened the fridge. It wasn't completely bare— there was enough stuff to throw together a basic meal if he got creative. "Did you eat?"

"You really are a mother hen. Yes, Gabe, I had dinner with Roxanne earlier. No, I'm not hungry. If you are, feel free to help yourself."

"You're so cute when you're patronizing me." He closed the door and pointed at the Benadryl. "Dose yourself."

She laughed. She had a really nice laugh. "Unbearably overbearing."

"There you go again, kicking me when I'm down." He waited until she took the meds and then cleaned out the little cup. "Now we can relax."

The living room was a nice surprise. He'd half-expected to find delicate ladylike furniture similar to something a grandmother would own, complete with doilies. Instead, there was an off-white sectional, huge and comfortable-looking. The television was a big screen, not as large as the mammoth one he had, but it wasn't something he'd be embarrassed to own. When he shot her a questioning look, she shrugged. "My brother picked it out."

He moved on to the case holding her DVD collection. Typical chick flicks and artsy types, but at the bottom he struck gold. *Rambo*. *Predator*. *Alien* and *Aliens*. All the *Terminator* movies. Looked like the princess had a thing for action movies.

"Don't judge me."

"Why would I judge you?" Gabe ran his finger along the titles, finding more favorites. *Die Hard. Demolition Man. Tremors.*

"There's nothing wrong with enjoying eighties action movies. They're classics."

"You say that like I'm arguing with you." Though obviously someone had—multiple someones from the way she automatically jumped on the defensive. "I happen to be into action flicks, eighties or otherwise."

She muttered something, and he finally tore his attention from the movies. "What?"

"Nothing." Elle sat, the very picture of innocence. She bit her lip when he pinned her with a look. "Okay, fine. I'm just kind of surprised we have something in common."

"We both like tattoos," he pointed out. "It was bound to happen again eventually."

She opened her mouth and then shut it. There was that blush again, right on cue. "You're just so…"

"Sexy. Charming."

"Overwhelming."

He decided on *Terminator 2: Judgment Day* and stuck the disc in the DVD player. "This is one of my favorites."

"Mine, too."

There was hope for them yet. But he had no intention of letting this conversation end. "You say I'm overwhelming like you're not sure if it's a good thing or a bad thing."

Elle already had the remotes ready when he settled in next to her. She tensed up for half a second, but finally relaxed against his side. He wanted to put his arm around her, but Gabe wasn't sure how she'd react.

"Well, I'm not sure. It's not like I expected this to happen when I crawled into bed that night." She paged through the menu and started the movie, oblivious to her affect on him. "I mean, we're just so different. Too different."

"You sound like you're trying to convince yourself."

"I don't have to convince myself of the truth. Look at me and look at you. God, that sounds so shallow, but you know what I mean. You hop around the West Coast, living the high life. I'm a freaking art curator for your brother."

"What's your point?"

"How can you even ask that?" She made a sound suspiciously close to a teakettle going off. "It's pretty freaking clear in my eyes. And, yeah, I know I didn't exactly give off the right impression when we, uh, met, but I don't do stuff like that.

Ever."

Gabe would have been blind not to figure that out for himself. No one wore crappy lingerie like that in real life, not to mention everything about her screamed sweet and innocent, even while she was coming around his fingers.

And he really shouldn't have let himself think that.

"I'm asking you again, because you still haven't given me a legit answer—what's your point?"

"My *point* is that you're obviously used to a different kind of female. One who wants the same things you do. I'm not her."

He would have laughed if he didn't feel like he'd stepped into the twilight zone. "You have some pretty hard-core ideas even though you've spent all of a few hours with me."

She went on as if he hadn't said anything. "I like my life. It's not exciting or anything, but it's mine. I want to settle down and have a family."

Wow, she really had the wrong idea about him. Okay, that wasn't exactly true. The guy she described *had* been Gabe—a few years ago. He'd been wild, but even then he hadn't partied like she seemed to think he did, and he sure as hell hadn't banged his way through an army of skanks either.

If he were going to be honest with her, with himself, he'd tell her that the life she just described was one he'd come to want more than anything else in the world in the last couple of years. But he couldn't force himself to give voice to the longing that left him breathless.

Besides, Elle obviously wasn't ready to hear about his past—or his future. When she started to talk again, Gabe pressed his finger to her lips and went with something to lighten the mood. "That night? That was some seriously terrible lingerie, babe."

She gasped. "It was not!"

"It really, really was."

"I'm not arguing with you about this right now, or ever." She shot up, horror widening her blue eyes. "Oh my God! I forgot to grab it before the cleaning crew showed up! They probably gave it to Nathan days ago." Her eyes watered and she buried her face in her hands. "If he finds out it's mine, he'll fire me for sure."

Gabe swallowed his guilt and spouted off another white lie. "They probably just threw it out. How about you just relax and stop thinking? Do you think you can manage that for one night?"

"No, I can't. It's like you haven't heard a single

thing I've said."

Yeah, he had, but he couldn't bear the thought of her being miserable after everything he'd put her through tonight. He pulled her hands away from her face. "Are you uncomfortable?"

Her blue eyes were wide as she shook her head. "Not particularly."

Gabe took a deep breath. "Do you want me to move?"

Again a pause, this one a little longer. He could almost see the battle between what she wanted and what she thought she should want. Finally, Elle shook her head again. Thank God. He didn't know if he had the strength to move to the other side of the couch right now. This next question was harder, but Gabe couldn't stand being this close and not at least asking. "Can I... hold you?"

"If you insist."

She was already burrowing into him by the time he got his arm up and over her. Christ, this felt good. Her head settled perfectly into the dip of his shoulder, giving him a whiff of her shampoo. "See, I'm not so bad."

Elle rolled her eyes. "I never said you were bad—just different."

"Different can be good."

"I thought you said I'm supposed to stop thinking."

"Touché." He could feel her smile against his chest. This was going to be one hell of a long night, but he'd known that going into it. One thing Gabe hadn't even managed to hope for was to have her here on the couch and in his arms. With them cuddling like this, he could almost pretend this little slice of domesticity wasn't just a fantasy. That he might really have a chance with Elle. "Get comfortable and let's watch Sarah Connor kick some ass."

After a brief hesitation, she slipped her arm over his stomach, her nails making his skin twitch, and gave a shuddery sigh. "Thank you for taking care of me, Gabe."

"Anytime, babe, any-freaking-time."

CHAPTER THIRTEEN

Elle snuggled up against a warm chest. A warm, very naked chest. Doing a quick mental inventory, she exhaled slowly when she realized all her clothes were firmly in place, right along with Gabe's sweatpants. Then again, why wouldn't they be? It wasn't like she blacked out last night or anything. Still, she couldn't be too careful. There had been more than one close call in the bathroom, and that was while she'd been suffering from a nasty allergic reaction.

Seriously, though, did he have to smell so damn good? And why was she lying on top of him? She turned her face into his chest and tried to pretend that she wasn't totally sniffing his skin. Not creepy at all. Right.

Gabe shifted and pulled her closer, one

hand settling on the small of her back, and the other cupping her neck. Like he cherished her or something. She sighed and ran a single finger over his skin, tracing the jagged line that bordered the tattoo stretching across the side of his chest, up his neck, and over his shoulder. The gears and pulleys were so incredibly intricate, they were almost lifelike. It was beautifully done, nothing like the vulgar stuff she'd seen before, stuff that was more branding than art.

What did Gabe's work look like? A few days ago, Nathan had mentioned that his brother owned a tattoo shop along with the nightclubs, but she'd dismissed the information as irrelevant.

Maybe there was more than one artist in the family.

"You're killing me, babe."

"I'm sorry." She froze, her finger less than an inch from his nipple.

"Don't be." He chuckled and pressed a kiss to her temple. "I'm not."

She lifted herself up so she could see his face, but the move shifted her body so that his erection was suddenly pushing against her lower stomach. Oh wow. Elle froze, torn between the desire to get off the couch and the need to rock against his length. Good God, did the man have a soft spot on his body? Even with her on top, she felt delicate, feminine, and completely out of control. Elle trembled when his one hand slid down to cup her behind.

He traced the thumb of his other hand over her bottom lip. "You really are gorgeous."

With him touching her like this, as if he really cared, she actually believed it was true. Even more than that, when Gabe said it, Elle felt like the most beautiful woman in the world. He must have seen something on her face, because Gabe pulled her up his body until his lips brushed her ear. "Don't look at me like that. Please."

"Why not?"

"Do you really want to know?"

At this angle, she couldn't see his face, wasn't sure she wanted to. Hell, Elle didn't know what she wanted in that moment. No, that was a lie. She'd wanted this from the beginning, but her need had doubled after their shared shower. Her lips moved of their own accord. "Yes."

His teeth closed over her earlobe, just shy of actual pain. Gabe soothed it with his tongue and then kissed down her neck. "Because when you look at me like that, all I can think about is getting you naked and tasting every inch of you."

Oh wow. Wait, this was bad. She was supposed

to be keeping her head around him. Right. She should get up. Or move. Or…something. "Every inch?"

"Yeah." His hand trailed up her back. "Down your spine." Gabe flipped her so Elle's back was pressed against his chest, his erection nestled against her bottom. She whimpered as both his hands dipped under her tank top, tracing over each place as he named it. "Around your hips— you have really sexy hip bones—and up your stomach."

He stopped just short of her breasts, his breath harsh in her ear. Elle thought she might scream if he didn't touch her, but she couldn't bring herself to say it. He knew though. His palms were rough against her nipples, and she arched her back, needing more.

"Gabe…"

"You have the most perfect breasts, and these nipples just beg to be teased." Too soon, his hands moved away, leaving her aching. "But, to tell you the truth, there's only one place I want my mouth right now."

It wasn't until he touched the waistband of her shorts that she understood. Again, he seemed to be waiting for her to…something. She had no idea. Elle couldn't think beyond the all-consuming need to have him touch her *there*.

With a curse, he slid one hand beneath the silk to cup her. She held her breath as he toyed with the edge of her panties before finally pulling them aside and then, lord, it was just his hands on her heated flesh.

A single finger traced her opening and, despite every effort to stay still, Elle couldn't help opening her legs a bit wider. Gabe pressed his forehead against her shoulder, his body shaking as his finger entered her. It wasn't enough, and when he withdrew, it pulled a whimper of protest from her.

Gabe's voice was so low and hoarse, she could barely hear him. "Once I was here, I'd take my time. I'd taste you, play with you, and when I finally let you come, you'd damn near black out."

Spreading her wetness, he found her clit, circling it and then withdrawing, before starting the process again. Over and over, as if he had all the time in the world.

Elle reached for him blindly, digging her nails into his upper arm. "Please."

He went still and she had the wild terror that he'd leave her like this, on the edge and nearly mad with wanting. But then he cursed again and plunged two fingers into her, using the heel of his palm to relentlessly drive her to oblivion.

"Oh, God, *Gabe*."

As the aftershocks hit her, he gentled his touch until it was almost too much to bear. He slid his hand out of her shorts and Elle turned in his arms, needing to touch him. "Just let me hold you for awhile, babe. Please."

Hold her? "But…" She could feel the length of him through his sweats—this had been completely one-sided. Again.

Gabe sat up with her in his lap and wrapped his arms more securely around her body. She wanted to argue, but the desire couldn't hold out against the languor spreading through her body in the aftermath. It was too good to be tangled up in him like this, especially after what was one of the single most erotic moments of her life. It wasn't a comfortable thought, but there it was.

She didn't know what to think about that.

• • •

He was hanging on by a thread. Gabe stroked her hair and mentally went through all the reasons having sex with Elle right now was a bad idea.

She was a good girl. After the time he'd spent with her, there was no getting around that fact.

Obviously, the night they met was a fluke. Not one he regretted, but definitely not the norm for her. This wasn't a woman who gave away her body without some intense strings attached.

Then again, he wanted those strings, wanted them badly. Gabe shifted his hold on her, running his hand down her legs and back up again. He wanted this woman with a passion he hadn't felt since opening his tattoo shop. It didn't make any sense. Two people could not be more different— or bicker more. Not to mention the fact she seemed determined to think the worst of him.

But, Christ, Gabe wanted to follow through on everything he'd told her he would do to her body. This chick had him so twisted up, he didn't know which way was north anymore. Maybe it wouldn't ruin this fragile peace they had going if he did it. They didn't have to have sex. Hell, she didn't have to do a damn thing except let him get her naked and go over her body for as long as he wanted to—which, at this point, would be hours.

Fuck it, he was going for it.

Gabe moved his hand down her leg again, this time rotating and coming up the inside of her thigh. Elle whimpered and spread her legs just enough that he could touch her through her shorts again. Well aware she might be overly sensitive after just coming, he kept it light, until she was making little movements, rubbing herself against him on the upstroke. He was pretty sure she had no idea she was doing it—and would have been horrified if she realized she was.

"Can I, babe?"

She looked over her shoulder at him, her lips just begging to be kissed. "Can you?"

"Will you"—he pressed a kiss to each corner of her mouth—"let me do what I just described?"

"*Oh.*" She bit her lip even as her hips kept up their steady movement. "Um...yes?"

The bottom of his stomach dropped out. "Yes?"

Elle nodded, not quite meeting his eyes. It was enough. He lifted her and set her on the couch, then slid backward, taking her shorts and panties off with him. Her face went crimson and she closed her legs, looking everywhere but at him. But she didn't scream bloody murder and demand he leave her house, so Gabe kissed her knee, nibbling until she giggled. "That tickles."

"Sorry."

"No, you're not."

He moved a little higher up her thigh and her breath hitched. It was slow going, but he wasn't going to dive on her like a starving man, even if that's how he felt right now. He nibbled and licked, each little sound she made unraveling his control further. Still, he held on. Finally, *finally*, Gabe settled between her thighs, right where he wanted to be. And, Christ, she was beautiful. Perfect.

The first swipe of his tongue earned a moan so loud, he was glad there was no one else in the house. It was his last thought before he gave himself over to the glory that was Elle. She trembled underneath his mouth, her body so responsive to his every touch that he wondered if anyone had done this for her before. The thought of being her first in this sent a possessive rush through him. And even if his wasn't the first mouth on her, he'd make damn sure she'd never forget about him.

Elle's hands crept into his hair, tentative at first, as if she thought he'd protest. When he sucked on her clit, her hips jerked and her hands held him in place, demanding more.

Distantly, a song started playing.

"*Oh my God.*"

Gabe stopped what he was doing and looked up. "What's wrong?"

"It's my phone."

"Ignore it."

She gasped when he gave her core another long lick and her hands spasmed on his head. "I can't think when you do that."

So, of course, he did it again. Gabe could ignore the ringing. Really, he could. And, from the way Elle's body was shaking, she was close to coming. He kept right on going as the blasted ringing stopped…and started right up again.

Gabe groaned. He recognized that ringtone. It was the same one from the bar, some old-school country song he vaguely recognized. "Please tell me that's not who I think it is."

"It's my mother's ringtone."

The same mother who'd obviously been harping on her when they were on their date. Great.

The ringing stopped and he hoped for a second that they could get back to business.

Elle gave a little scream when her phone started up again. "*Seriously*?"

Gabe pressed his forehead to her stomach and sighed. "I think we're going to need to pick this up later, babe." In the meantime, he needed a goddamn icy shower again.

CHAPTER FOURTEEN

Elle hopped on one foot as she yanked her shorts back on and ran for the kitchen, leaving Gabe on the couch. She took a deep breath as she picked up the phone and tried to sound like she hadn't just been on the verge of orgasming. "Hello?"

"Ellie, what in God's name took you so long? You can't possibly still be sleeping. It's nine o'clock in the morning. "

She cast a guilty look toward the living room door and moved farther into the kitchen. "Hey, Mom. I was just cleaning."

"Are you okay? You sound odd."

Odd didn't begin to cover it. Elle's entire body was strung so tightly she wanted to scream. And not in a good way. Thankfully, there was nothing quite like the fear of God to douse any remaining desire she had. "Yes, I'm fine."

"I see." She didn't sound convinced, but apparently it was a good enough answer because she started rambling about her and Dad's upcoming trip to Maryland. Elle listened with half an ear, murmuring yes and no when needed, but the rest of her attention was trying to pinpoint what Gabe was doing.

Was he mad? She hoped not. Maybe it would have been better to let the phone go to voice mail again, but she'd never been able to do that, especially with her mother—especially since the woman refused to leave a message. Instead, she preferred to keep calling until Elle picked up. Footsteps thudded above her head and the shower turned on. Elle exhaled, relief and disappointment warring inside her.

"Ellie, are you listening to me?"

"What? Of course I am."

Her mom sighed. "No, you're not. I take the time out of my morning to try and talk to you, and you're completely distracted. What's going on?"

For one panicked moment, she was sure her mom knew everything. Elle bit her lip, pushing down the insane urge to confess. "Nothing, Mom. I'm just cleaning. The house is a sty."

"You know we've talked about this—you need to put more effort keeping up your home. Good God, what if a man comes over and sees how disgusting it is?"

Considering there was a man here right now, she didn't think her "disgusting" house would be a deal-breaker. Gabe wasn't the type to care if things were immaculate. And, seriously, did she want to end up with a man who obsessed about things like that? Elle took a deep breath. "That's why I'm cleaning."

Her mom huffed. "At least you're being proactive. I've set up a welcome home dinner for Ian when your father and I get back from Maryland, and I'd like you to come."

That invitation should have gone without saying. Her mother was up to something. "What aren't you telling me?"

"You're being unforgivably rude right now, young lady."

And she was avoiding the question. "*Mom.*"

"Oh, fine, if you insist. I've invited Sammy as well."

She so couldn't deal with talking about another man when her legs were still shaking from the almost-orgasm. "I have to go. We're talking about this later."

"I don't know what's gotten into you, Ellie, but I am not impressed. I'm only trying to do what's best for you. I want you happy."

Happy? Yeah, right. She'd be horrified if she knew what Elle had just been doing, regardless of how happy it had been on the verge of making her. "I know. I love you too. Bye, Mom."

Elle set the phone on the counter. What should she do now? The smart thing would be to go tidy up the living room and wait for Gabe to finish with the shower, but there was a part of her that wanted to meet him upstairs and see if he'd finish what he started.

Bad idea. Really bad idea. If they started up again, there was no way they'd stop. She lost her mind when he had his hands on her—let alone his mouth—and it was all too easy for things to get carried away.

But would that really be so bad?

Elle spun her phone, thinking back over the night. From the time he handed her the flowers to when they passed out in each other's arms, he hadn't done a single thing to send off her internal alarms. In fact, he'd gone out of his way to take care of her. The chicken noodle soup and chocolate on the counter were testament enough of that—not to mention the underhanded way he'd forced the Benadryl on her. Actually, even though it pissed her off at the time, looking back it was kind of cute.

All of it added up to the conclusion that maybe she'd been wrong. Oh God, she was afraid to even hope the man he'd been for the last twelve hours was the truth.

Footsteps pounded down the stairs and Gabe came into view, wearing only his jeans from last night. He held up his shirt. "I figured we'd better not tempt fate."

The sage. Right.

He tossed it into the hall by the front door and quickly washed his hands. Elle didn't move, not sure how to take him being so normal after what they were just doing. Were they just going to pretend it didn't happen?

"Do you want to talk about it?"

Elle blinked. "Talk about it?"

"You were kind of frazzled after the last conversation you had with your mom." He made a show of looking her over. "You have that same look in your eye now."

"I'm not sure what to say." She pulled herself onto the counter and sighed. "It's just family stuff."

He smiled, the easygoing expression making

her stomach tumble head over heels. "So tell me about your family."

"What do you want to know?"

"Everything."

"I have an older brother." She wrinkled her nose. "He's kind of a pain sometimes. Ian's in the army and, right now, he's stationed in Japan." Truth be told, she kind of missed him, even if Ian was overbearing as all get-out.

Gabe nodded as if she'd just confirmed something. "You're close to your parents."

It wasn't a question, but she answered anyway. "Yes. They live up on the South Hill, but we try to do dinner at least once a week." Enough about her—she wanted to know more about him. Elle drummed her fingers on the countertop, wondering if he'd shoot her questions down. Nathan didn't like to talk about his family, and she didn't see Gabe being any different.

He eyed her hand's restless movement. "Ask."

"I know you have Nathan." Which still weirded her out a little bit, if she were going to be honest. "Any other siblings?"

"Nope. Just us two."

It was probably a good thing. She didn't think her world could handle another Schultz sibling, especially a brother. "What happened with your parents?" Because they weren't around anymore, she was sure of it.

Gabe dug through her cupboards, almost fidgeting. She waited, unwilling to press him. Either he'd open up to her or he wouldn't, but she couldn't force this.

He inhaled so deeply she could actually hear it, almost as if he were preparing for a fight. "It's your typical sob story. Dad was a drunk who liked to smack us around when he was there—which wasn't often. Couldn't hold down a job and liked to take his frustration out on our mom. Finally up and took off without so much as a good-bye and left Mom to take care of two kids she could barely support."

Elle swallowed the sympathetic words threatening to come out of her mouth. From the look on his face, he wouldn't appreciate them. But, God, she couldn't imagine growing up like that, without the loving—okay, infuriating—support of her family. She bit her lip and stayed silent, waiting for him to continue.

"She made it all the way until I graduated high school. Nathan was just a year behind me, a senior at the time. One day Mom was fine and the next we got a call from the hospital saying she'd had a heart attack."

He cleared his throat, staring off into the distance, his mind obviously years in the past. "I…I honestly don't know how we got through it. I was working two jobs and Nathan quit football and got one of his own. He wanted to drop out, but I'd be damned before I let him shit away his diploma. Mom wouldn't have wanted it. It wasn't easy, but he got through graduation and joined the army. And then, one day out of the blue, a lawyer showed up on our doorstep with a will for Dad. Guess he drank himself to death or something, but he'd had a shit-ton of family money none of us ever knew about."

There was a world of condemnation in his tone. She knew what he was thinking—that money might have made the difference with his mother. Unable to hold back any longer, Elle slid off the counter and crossed the kitchen to stand before him. She opened her arms, offering the support she knew he wouldn't take in words. Gabe pulled her against him, wrapping her up as if he were the one comforting her. Heck, maybe he was.

"So what about you? What's your deal with your parents?"

Elle gave her cop-out answer without thinking

about it. "The norm."

"Forgive me, but bullshit."

She wasn't sure she liked being the sole recipient of his attention, but Gabe shared his story. Could she do any less? Besides, it was easier to talk if she wasn't looking at his face. "I love them, but... My dad is laid back, almost too laid back. My mom walks all over him—over all of us. She's intense."

It seemed like a really pathetic thing to whine about after what he'd told her, but Gabe didn't sneer or roll his eyes when he pulled away. Instead, he watched her intently. With a deep breath, she kept talking. "I just—I don't know. I'll never be good enough in her eyes, never get the right job, marry the right man, pick the life she wants for me."

"I don't know your mom, but from what I've seen, you know your own mind. You, Elle Walser, are a woman to be proud of."

She smiled. "And you, Gabe Schultz, are a good man."

• • •

A good man?

Gabe stared at Elle, pretty damn sure his

mouth was hanging open. Had she really just said that? "You really think I'm a good man?"

She smiled so sweetly his heart gave an odd thump. "I know it."

He cupped her face, marveling that this was happening, that this woman was really standing here after hearing his sob story, not a trace of pity in her eyes or any of the disgust he'd figured she'd always felt for him. Instead there was... admiration?

There was nothing else to do but kiss her. Gabe pressed his lips to hers, trying to make her understand how much her words and understanding meant to him. More than he could possibly express aloud.

As his tongue traced her bottom lip, she opened to him. No hesitation. No holding back. Elle melted in his arms with a whimper. He pulled back enough to say, "I want to finish what we started on the couch."

Elle nodded. "Yes, yes, so much yes."

Answer enough. For half a second, he considered setting her on the counter and tasting her right here—he was dying to have her come against his face—but it didn't seem right. Not after what they'd just shared. So Gabe swept her into his arms and headed for her bedroom. With her pressing kisses against his neck, he took the stairs three at a time, needing to have her naked and under him.

He stopped at the foot of her bed and set her on her feet. They stared at each other for one eternal moment. This was actually happening. He could barely believe it was real, but he wasn't going to let this experience be anything less than perfect.

"I love this tattoo." Elle ran her hand over his pecs and down his side. With a quick glance at him, she ducked down and flicked her tongue along the edge of his tat. "I've wanted to do that ever since I saw it."

Hell, she could do that any time she wanted. Gabe laced his fingers through her hair and tugged her back up for another kiss. He coaxed her mouth open and teased her tongue until she was writhing against him. Slow. No matter how much he wanted to pin her against the wall and take her hard, this was going to go slow.

He skimmed off her tease of a tank top and made short work of her shorts. Then there was only Elle, naked as the day he'd met her. If he'd thought she was a fantasy woman before, the feeling was only so much stronger now.

With her damned Cupid's bow offering too

much temptation, Gabe nipped her upper lip and then soothed the spot with his tongue. Elle laced her arms around his neck, the position leaving her entire body available for his exploration. But Gabe needed her on the bed to take full advantage of it. With another lingering kiss, he nudged her until the back of her thighs hit the mattress. "Lie down."

Instantly, she obeyed. Gabe stopped her before she could scoot out of reach, taking hold of her knees. Using only the slightest of pressure, he coaxed her legs open. Even from this distance, he could see how wet she was. For *him*.

"There are no words to describe this." Gabe ran his hands down over her calves and up her shins, pausing over her knees when she giggled. "Gorgeous. Beautiful. Fucking indescribable."

"Gabe…" She bit her lip, not quite meeting his eyes.

He nibbled up her thigh. A shuddery sigh was her only response. Well, that, and Elle widening her legs to give him better access. Gabe dipped a finger into her wetness, drawing a quick circle around her clit. "I'm going to say something, but please don't take it the wrong way."

Elle went tense as if expecting a blow. Which made him wonder *why* she'd be expecting it, but

Gabe let the thought go. It was something to dwell over later. He drew another circle around her clit. "I could spend days with my mouth between your legs, and never be satisfied."

Her shocked gasp turned into a moan when he kissed her there, using his tongue to explore every inch of her. Who was he kidding? Days would never be enough. Already the taste of her was an addiction, something he would never get enough of.

• • •

Having this man's mouth on her was enough to make Elle lose her mind. Like before, on the couch, Gabe took his time exploring her, as if he spoke the truth when he said he could go on for days.

She didn't know if she could survive days of this. It was too good. Elle never lost control, never was anything less than poised and polished. And yet out of control was all she'd been since that first night with Gabe. She couldn't stop herself from lacing her fingers through his hair and riding his mouth, desperate for more, for less, for *something*.

Her orgasm bowed her back, and Elle

shrieked, her nails digging into his scalp and holding him in place. For his part, Gabe didn't stop, teasing out the aftershocks until she wasn't sure she could remember her name. She started to push him away, body screaming that it was too much, but somehow he knew and pulled back to nibble his way up and over her hip bones.

"I'll never get enough of that."

Never? The word would've terrified her if she could string a single thought together. Instead, Elle held him close as her body shook. Gabe traced a wandering path over her skin, running his hands over her until she'd recovered enough to touch him back. And how much had she wanted to do exactly this ever since they met? More than Elle cared to admit. She explored his broad shoulders, the large arms that had no difficulty sweeping her off her feet, the body she'd begun to paint.

Finally, he pressed her forehead to hers, his ragged breaths almost a perfect match for her own. "I'm going to ask you a question, and I want you to be honest with me."

More questions? Elle didn't know if she could handle much more. "Yes?"

"Will you let me make love to you?"

There was no question. None of her worries or fears could hold up to the desire beating in time with her racing heart. Unwilling to give herself the opportunity to sound like an idiot, she only nodded.

"Are you sure?"

She could have laughed at the repeat of their first exchanged words. But things were different now and, as unsure as she'd been that first night, there was no room for doubts here. "I'm sure."

Gabe pushed off her so fast, she had a terrified second of thinking he was playing with her. But then she caught sight of him rifling through his wallet. He came up with a silver wrapper, looking all too pleased with himself. "You forgot something in your mad dash to get away from me that first time."

She had, hadn't she? Elle shook her head and held her arms out. Instead of obeying, he grinned at her and unzipped his jeans. Watching him slip out of them was way sexier than she could have imagined, but apparently Elle's imagination had been seriously lacking all these years. Gabe ripped open the condom and rolled it on, his hand sliding over his length. "Last chance, babe. Say you're not ready and we're done. No pressure."

"Shut up and get over here."

He chuckled and crawled onto the bed, settling between her legs. If Elle had thought they'd get to it, she was sorely disappointed. Gabe kissed her slowly, thoroughly, his tongue lazily twirling around hers. When she finally angled her hips, unable to wait another second to have him inside her, he reached between them. Then he was there, the broad head of his cock pressed against her entrance. He worked into her slowly, giving her body plenty of time to accommodate him.

Finally, Elle had had enough. She dug her nails into his butt hard enough that he jerked, slamming the rest of the way in. They froze, their bodies as close as two people could be. A nearly overwhelming wave of emotion rolled over her when Gabe propped himself up on his elbows and met her gaze. He looked down to where they were joined and a muscle in his jaw ticked. "Fuck, Elle."

Using the barest of movements, he rolled his hips, rubbing against the same spot his fingers had unerringly found before. Elle moaned as she arched to meet him. Already pressure was building, a wave cresting on the horizon. She caught Gabe watching her as if he were memorizing her face, but there was no time to worry about it because the wave rolled over her, sucking her under. How had she never known it could be like this? Elle bit his shoulder, trying to muffle her moans. Gabe's rhythm grew jagged, rougher, as he shoved his way into her again and again. She could only cling to him as he shuddered, gathering her close.

With a final groan, Gabe collapsed, rolling off her in nearly the same movement. She stared at the ceiling, her breath coming in harsh gasps, and smiled when his fingers laced with hers. Sometime later, he cleared his throat. "Does this mean you'll go out with me again?"

Elle didn't even have to think about it. "Yes. Yes, it does."

Chapter Fifteen

"Tell me *everything*."

Elle balanced the phone as she elbowed her way out of her house. She didn't want to deal with Roxanne freaking out, but it was better than her showing up here, demanding answers. "There's nothing much to tell." Nothing except Gabe giving her one of the best orgasms of her life on her couch, and then spending the day making her lose her mind in bed. On top of that, he promised a date to remember this weekend. But she could hardly tell Roxanne all that.

"Baloney. And you didn't tell me how gorgeous he is in that roughed-up sorta way. What happened after he hauled you out of here? Because I half thought he was going to toss you over his shoulder like a caveman if you didn't go willingly."

Elle rolled her eyes. "It wasn't anything like that." Yes, it had been. She could still see the expression on his face when he told her to take the Benadryl or he was going to force her to. Gabe wasn't someone to be messed with. Funny how that used to turn her off and now she thought it was hotter than hell.

"Now you're just teasing me. Spill."

There was no getting around this, no matter how much she wanted to. But she had to talk about it with someone, and Ian wasn't around. Not that Elle had ever been able to talk to him about guys. Because, seriously, he'd almost killed Jason after he found out they had sex. She shuddered to remember the look on her brother's face before he'd gotten in his truck and driven away. Next thing they knew, the cops were showing up with him in the backseat. Not exactly the brightest moment of her college career.

"Are you still there?"

She shook her head to clear away the memories. "Yeah, sorry. Just had a weird thought."

"Focus on me, the one who's dying to know what happened last night. Come on!"

"Okay, fine. He dragged me to the grocery store, bought a bunch of stuff that I didn't need,

and then drove me home and refused to leave."
When Roxanne gave a shuddery sigh, Elle pulled
her phone away from her face and frowned. "Are
you okay?"

"Yes, I'm fine. Keep going. What happened
next?"

"Next…" Her phone beeped. Elle looked at
it again and a stupid grin spread across her face.
Gabe. "Rox, I'm going to have to call you back.
Talk to you later." She switched over, cutting off
her friend's protest. "Hello?"

"Hey, beautiful."

Butterflies erupted in her stomach and her
heart skipped a beat. All from a single word.
"How are you doing this morning?"

"Could be better."

"Is something wrong?" God, what if he was
having second thoughts about taking her out
again?

Gabe laughed. "Just that I didn't wake up
with a sexy blonde in my arms. Know anyone
who fits the bill?"

She didn't know what to do with this casual
flirting. Elle swallowed, trying to find something
witty to say in response. "Not so much." Oh, that
was great. Now he was going to think she was
fishing for a compliment—*Oh please, won't you*

tell me I'm pretty? Ugh. Better change the subject before this got even more uncomfortable. "So what are you up to today?"

"Nathan's dragging me out to Clayton for lunch."

"Clayton?" There wasn't anything out that way but endless fields and a lone trailer park as far as she knew. Sure, Loon Lake was a few miles past, but if they were going there, Gabe would have said so.

Once again, she was hit with a longing for a beach. Maybe she should scrap her plans to run errands and head out to the lake for a few hours… It was an irresponsible thing to do, but she couldn't shake the urge.

"You mean you aren't aware of the Clayton Burger? Woman, you have got to get out more. It's the single most disgustingly fantastic creation in the area—a burger with a hot dog. The best of both worlds."

She made a face. "Sounds…appetizing."

"Yeah, it's not really your thing. I get that." He laughed again. "What are you doing this afternoon? Can I see you again?"

Elle pressed a hand to her mouth. Yep, the stupid grin just got wider. What was it about this guy who made her feel so out of control? The free-falling sensation should have sent her into full on panic mode, but all she felt was giddy.

"I have half a million things that need to be taken care of in town. Honestly, though, I'm kind of thinking about playing hooky and going to Loon Lake."

"Let's do it. I'll grab some beer and meet you there. Or do you like those wine cooler things?"

Screw errands—she was going to the lake with Gabe. "If you get Blue Moon, I'm good."

"Consider it done."

"What about Nathan?" She didn't want him to ditch his brother to hang out with her, especially not after what he'd told her yesterday. And, honestly, she wasn't sure how she felt about Nathan now in general. Elle had been so certain he was the man for her, but then Gabe showed up and blindsided her. He made her feel so much. Far more than Nathan ever had. But that didn't mean she wanted to mess with their brotherly bonding time.

"Oh, I'll give him a heads-up. He can come, too, if he wants."

Elle tripped over the bottom step of her porch. "Come too?"

"Yeah, why not?"

Because she didn't know how to deal with

being around them both at the same time? Obviously Nathan knew something was up, or he wouldn't have practically shoved her into Gabe's arms, but... What if Gabe told him about last week—and last night? How was she supposed to look Nathan in the face?

Gabe continued on, oblivious to her inner turmoil. "Meet you there at noon?"

She glanced at her watch. Plenty of time to change and get up there. "Sure."

"Good. See you soon."

Elle made her way to her bedroom, wondering how she got herself into these messes. It seemed to be an ongoing thing where Gabe was concerned. One minute she was on the straight and narrow, her path laid out in front of her, and the next she was flying down a rabbit trail, without supplies, and completely lost.

Okay, yeah, she just went off the deep end with the metaphor.

She put on her bright pink bikini and cover-up. Elle paused in front of her floppy hat. It was a silly thing, but she loved it. And, heck, she was so fair that skin cancer was a very real concern... but it wasn't sexy. She frowned. Was she seriously thinking about not wearing this hat just because it was more suited to a grandma than a sex goddess? No, just no. He could take it or leave it, but this was her, right along with all her other quirks.

Funny how her mental rant didn't do a single thing to calm her stomach as she shoved the hat into her beach bag. Right next to her sunscreen, towel, and steamy romance novel. Elle dropped the bag on the bed before she could start messing with its contents, and went searching for her beach flip-flops. She slipped them on, wiggling her toes. They needed another coat of polish, but there wasn't time and the sand played havoc on it anyway.

Enough with the second-guessing. It was time to leave. Sure, she'd get up there early, but there was nothing wrong with that. This way she could take some time to zone out with her book. It had been so long since Elle relaxed she wasn't even sure where she left off with the story. Maybe she should just start from the beginning again.

She grabbed her bag and a bottle of water and left. The drive passed quickly, and she eyed Clayton as she flew past. There was a ramshackle building that must be the restaurant, but she never would have guessed just by looking at it. There wasn't even a sign. Thank God Gabe hadn't invited her along to lunch. She wasn't sure she would get past the front door.

Elle paid the five-dollar fee to get into the park and then made her way down to the rickety stairs. She passed directly in front of the huge U-shaped dock where all the kids were playing, and picked a spot on the second, smaller beach. It was mostly empty, but for a middle-aged couple.

After rubbing every exposed inch of her skin with sunscreen, Elle stripped off the cover-up and lay on her stomach, romance novel open in front of her. The floppy hat provided just enough shade to counteract the glare of the pages, and she promptly got lost in the story of a Highlander and his reluctant bride.

Things were so much simpler in romance novels, when she knew that—no matter what trials they went through—there was a happily-ever-after waiting for the couple involved. Real life was rarely so simple.

CHAPTER SIXTEEN

Gabe almost tripped over his own feet when he caught sight of Elle in her pink bikini and grandma hat. She was completely focused on the book in her hands, and he could make a pretty decent guess to the contents based on the shirtless guy on the cover. So she liked romance books—good to know she wasn't immune to every so-called "trashy" thing.

He was tempted to stand there and watch her until she noticed him, but that was a creeper thing to do. So Gabe dropped into the sand next to her and grinned. "Hey."

"I didn't even see you walk up." She slammed the book closed and shoved it into her bag. "Where's Nathan?"

Irrational jealousy surged, so strong he

actually saw red for half a second before Gabe fought for control. "He had a few things to take care of, but then he'll be up here." Though he was suddenly wishing Nathan wouldn't show. Damn it, no. He was not going to be jealous.

Instead of looking disappointed, she smiled, brighter than the sun above them. "Okay."

He needed to change the subject now, before he did something stupid like ask her if she still wanted his little brother. "What are you reading?"

"Nothing." She edged the bag to the far side of her body, which only made his curiosity perk up. "Just a book."

"Cool." Gabe waited until she relaxed, obviously thinking he'd lost interest, before he leaned over her back and snagged the bag. Elle gave a little shriek and dove for it, but he easily kept it out of reach. And, hell, he could play this game of keep-away forever if it meant he had her squirming in his lap.

He lifted the bag over his head and she lunged, her boobs hitting him in the face. Yeah, he was totally okay with this. He used his free hand to tickle Elle's side, and she smacked him, still trying to grab the bag. "Give it back."

"What's this book about, anyway?" He

switched his grip and swung it behind his back. She started to go after it and then froze. Apparently she'd finally realized what their wrestling match was doing to him and, considering she was now straddling his hips, he'd bet she wasn't completely unaffected either.

"Um."

Elle started to slide off his lap, but Gabe hooked an arm around her waist, keeping her in place. "I like you here."

"People can *see* us." She pulled her hat further down on her head, as if that would make a difference.

Gabe leaned in until his cheek brushed hers and lowered his voice. "We're not having sex, babe." Though that could change with a quick jerk of their swimsuits. Not that he'd do that, not in the middle of the day where there were kids running around. He'd take her out to one of the hiking trails around Coeur d'Alene Lake some night, though, and then they'd see if her desire overrode her reservations.

"*Gabe.*" He let go and it wasn't until she was safely back on her towel that her head whipped around. "My book."

"Finder's keepers." Gabe flipped it open to a random place and scanned the page. "Holy shit."

"Give it back."

She made as if she was going to grab it, but he held up his hand, still reading. "This is pretty hot."

"I—what?"

"I mean, I'm not normally into the whole historical thing, but damn, babe." She obviously had great taste in more than just tattoos. When her mouth dropped open, he waggled his eyebrows at her over his sunglasses. "Want to read it aloud and then try this position out?"

It was hard to tell in the bright light, but he was pretty sure she turned crimson. "I can't believe you just said that."

Considering where his mouth had been just a little over twenty-four hours ago, he was surprised by her shyness. Then again, this was Elle—it was entirely possible she'd never had an explicit conversation in her life. He caught himself wondering if she'd ever watched porn and killed the thought. Doubtful. Really doubtful.

But, Christ, she hadn't been shy in bed. Not that she was brazen by any means, but Elle had a way about her. It made him desperate to take her again and again, until they'd both been so exhausted they could only lie intertwined and breathe. All in all, one of the best days he'd had in as long as he could remember.

Gabe handed the book back. "I like your style."

"You're incorrigible."

"Only most days." He stretched, enjoying the feel of the sun on his skin. Between the lapping of waves created by passing boats and the scattered laughter of the kids on the next beach over, Gabe finally started to relax. It'd been a long time since he unwound. Forever, really.

But there was something about this chick that made it possible. He reached over and laced his hand with hers. "Thanks for coming."

"Thanks for inviting yourself." She laughed. "But I'm glad we did this."

Gabe was too. "You want a beer?"

"Sure." Elle accepted the bottle and took a tentative sip. "I don't normally like beer, but this kind always does it for me."

"You've never been to a brewery, have you?" When she shook her head, he sighed. "It's a totally different experience. We'll have to go sometime. There's a new little one that opened up in the valley—amazing beer. I think we could find something you'd enjoy."

Using her finger to trace a pattern in the sand, she seemed to look everywhere but at him.

"You seem to be making all kinds of plans like that."

"Plans like what?"

"You know, for the future."

Gabe sat back and watched her fidget. At what point did he tell her he had no intention of going anywhere? That he wanted to see if they really could have a future? He sipped his beer. "Babe, you're overthinking again. Are you having a good time right now?"

"Yes." Her voice was small, as if admitting something embarrassing.

"And do you think going to a brewery could be fun?" When she shrugged, he laughed. "It's nothing like Lou's—very clean-cut and reputable. I promise you'd approve."

A smile finally pulled at the edges of her mouth. "I'm pretty transparent, huh?"

No, but it seemed the majority of the things he enjoyed, she'd be horrified by. They shared a love of art and crappy eighties action movies, though. And tattoos, too, apparently, which was even more important than the rest. Relationships had been built on less. Not to mention the future she'd painted was one he wanted more than anything. So what if they were exact opposites in some ways? It just made life more interesting.

Gabe made a mental note not to take her into another of his dive bars for the time being. Maybe later on... Maybe not. He'd have to play it by ear. Thinking back to the romance novel, he grinned. "So Highlanders are your thing?"

"We're so not talking about this."

He moved closer, skating a hand up her leg. "Are you sure? Because I'd be more than happy to kidnap you and blackmail you into being my secret sex slave."

"That's not what the book's about." Elle shook her head and laughed. "You're being outrageous."

"You like it." He cupped her through her bikini, earning a sharp inhale.

"Someone will see." Even as she spoke, she pressed against him.

The summery scent of suntan lotion had never smelled as good as it did on her skin. Smiling to himself, Gabe nibbled on her earlobe. "No one can see what I'm doing to you, babe. Which means I can do anything I want." With a quick move, he slipped his hand into her swimsuit, finding her hot and soaking wet. "I think that novel got you all worked up."

This time her laugh was tinged with desperation. "*Gabe.*"

"I really like it when you say my name." He plunged two fingers into her and Elle gasped. "Better not moan. Someone will hear you."

"Oh, God."

Searching for a better angle, Gabe pressed the heel of his hand against her clit as he fucked her with his fingers. "They won't know, though, as long as you scream into my mouth when you come."

She leaned more heavily against him, her hands creating furrows in the sand. Little sounds slipped from her lips even as she so obviously fought to stay quiet. Holy shit, if there was anything sexier than Elle about to come, Gabe had no idea what it was.

Just as her body tightened with the beginnings of what he had no doubt would be an explosive orgasm, the roar of a diesel engine intruded. Sure, it could be anyone, but Gabe had never been that lucky, which meant Nathan was here. He glanced up to see the big black truck pulling into a parking space at the top of the stairway. They had two minutes, at best, before Nathan showed up. Fuck it, he was going to make his woman come, his brother be damned.

But Elle shoved his hand away. "Nathan's here." Without another word, she pushed to her feet and started for the water.

Gabe lost his train of thought in the face of the tiny string bikini that barely covered her ass. For such a square, she sure as hell liked clothes that drove men wild. Then again, with Elle, it was entirely possible she had no idea what she was doing to him. With a groan, he got up and followed her. Maybe the cold temperature of the lake would be enough to cool his desire.

Yeah, somehow he doubted it.

• • •

Elle didn't know what to think. Okay, that was a lie. She knew exactly what to think. But part of her rebelled against the overwhelming feeling of *rightness* she experienced whenever she was around Gabe. Even now, knee-deep in cold water, she was half-tempted to throw caution to the wind and jump into his arms. He'd catch her—there was no doubt about it.

There should be doubt. She'd only known him a week. Sure, it'd been a really intense week, but it was still only a week. It shouldn't matter that he made her body sing, not when she'd already proved how poor a judge her body was. Look at what she'd just been doing—getting frisky on a freaking public beach. And yet… Elle had never felt so alive in her life.

One could argue that it was strictly the post-sex high making her head fuzzy, but she didn't think so. They hadn't had sex since yesterday, after all. Maybe she just didn't care. Gabe held her, touched her, kissed her as if he cared. Really cared. No one could fake something on that level. She was sure of it.

"What's going on in that pretty head of yours?"

Elle adjusted her hat in the breeze that kicked up over the water. "Just thinking." Before he could ask her what, she looked past him and blurted, "There's Nathan."

But the relief at getting out of their current conversation was dwarfed by the sudden realization she was actually going to have to spend time with both Gabe and Nathan. At the same time.

It wasn't too late. She could pretend she was sick and bolt. Elle slanted a glance at Gabe and sighed. If he thought she was sick, he'd want to go with her and make sure she was okay or, worse, threaten to drag her to the hospital. Again. No, she was going to have to keep her chin up and get through this afternoon. How bad could it be?

Nathan stopped next to their towels long

enough to strip off his shirt. Elle tried to keep her jaw from dropping.

"Try not to drool on yourself, babe." Though Gabe's voice was light, his mouth thinned.

God, did he think she was checking out his brother? Okay, so Nathan was just as good-looking as she'd imagined, but that wasn't the point. He had *tattoos*. Not as many as Gabe, but enough that she couldn't stop staring. "Nathan has *tattoos*."

"Uh, yeah. What did you expect?"

She didn't have time to answer because Nathan had already made his way into the water. Seeing the brothers side by side without her anger blinding her to the details, Elle was positive she was going to pass out. They were really more similar than she'd first thought. And...*the tattoos*.

She'd tried so hard to pick a refined man her mother would approve of, and she'd failed miserably. Her Mr. Right radar was seriously broken.

"Hey, Elle. Gabe."

Right, so this wasn't awkward at all. "Hey. So...how are you?" What a question to ask. She'd just seen him two days ago. But everything seemed different now, especially after what happened between her and Gabe—and what he'd told her about their family. Elle just wanted to give them both a hug, which was a terrible idea. Good lord, she needed another beer.

Nathan's gaze jumped between her and Gabe, his smile spreading into an all-out grin. "Obviously not as good as you two."

Oh my God. Nathan *knew*. Which meant he knew she'd snuck into Nathan's loft with the intention of seducing *him*. Elle couldn't breathe even though her lungs were screaming for air.

Gabe must have picked up on her discomfort because he smacked Nathan in the shoulder, a little too hard to be strictly playful—or maybe that was her imagination talking. "Yeah, well, you win some and you lose some. I won this one."

"Right place, right time."

How could they be joking at a time like this? She was pretty sure the world was ending. And, yep, she was going to pass out. If things worked out, maybe she'd drown before one of them grabbed her and save herself from this embarrassment.

"Are you okay?" Gabe touched her shoulder as the world started to go white around the edges. "Babe, breathe."

Déjà vu hit her so hard she nearly collapsed. He'd said the same freaking thing to her the night

she was *supposed* to be having sex with Nathan.
Funny, but it didn't seem to work any better this
time around. She swayed, putting some serious
consideration into swimming until she couldn't
swim anymore and then letting the dark water
take her. Drowning was supposed to be peaceful,
right? She'd read that somewhere. Or maybe
that was freezing to death? Heck, there had to
be a freezer somewhere she could crawl into.
Anything was better than standing here and
having this conversation.

"What's wrong with her?"

"I don't know." Gabe shook her and, darn
it, startled her into a huge inhale. "There you go.
What's wrong?"

"Nathan knows," she croaked.

The brothers exchanged a look and Nathan
laughed. "Elle, I've known since that night. You
left your…whatever the hell it is in my loft."

All this time, and neither one of them had
said a thing. Worse, Gabe had lied to her face
about it. She jerked out of Gabe's grip and
smacked him. "What the heck is wrong with you?
Why didn't you tell me?"

"Probably because you'd react like this?"

Nathan shrugged and smiled. "It's really not
a big deal."

It felt like the top of her head exploded right then and there. She glared at her boss. "*Not a big deal?*"

His grin faltered. "Is it a big deal? You aren't going to quit, are you?"

Good God, one brother was just as bad as the other. Elle wanted to strangle them, both standing there, their confusion written all over their faces. Of course they wouldn't see what the big deal was. This kind of thing happened *all the time* in real life. Yeah, right. "I cannot believe you two."

"I'm sorry, babe." For his part, Gabe actually looked it. "But how was I supposed to find out who you were if I didn't talk to Nathan about it?"

"But...he *knows*." Her mind couldn't get past that single thing. Nathan knew she'd been naked and intimate with his brother. His freaking brother. It wasn't like she still wanted him after all this, but it didn't lessen the embarrassment one iota.

"It's really okay." How Nathan could sound so calm and rational right now was beyond her. She just wanted to curl up and die. And he just kept right on talking. "I think it's great that it happened. You guys are really good together."

Elle blinked. "What?"

"I'm serious." Nathan elbowed his brother. "I haven't seen Gabe this happy in ages."

"I'm standing right here—and you're not helping." He took her arm and pulled her away, out of the water and back onto the beach. "Babe, are you okay? Do you want to go?"

Looking into his concerned face, some of her anxiety melted away. "He's really known this entire time?"

"Yeah. Like I said, I'm sorry."

Nathan had known she almost slept with his brother and didn't care. Heck, if he was okay with it, he was probably relieved she hadn't found the right bed. That should have hurt, but now that she wasn't freaking out, all she felt was a curious relief. Maybe she'd been so focused on finding a man her mother would approve of she'd been trying to force something that shouldn't be forced. Air rushed into her lungs as her panic attack dissipated. Elle forced a smile, even though it wobbled a bit around the edges. "It's... okay."

"Are you sure?"

"Yeah." And, oddly enough, she was.

CHAPTER SEVENTEEN

The last thing Gabe wanted to deal with was his ringing phone. Again. He'd stopped by his office to fax a few things to the Portland club, and it was like the universe was waiting to pounce on him. Two hours later and he was no closer to leaving.

With a sigh, he picked up the phone. "Schultz here."

"You're avoiding my calls."

The universe really did hate him. "Lynn."

"Look, I get it. You don't want to deal with this asshole. Guess what? I don't want to deal with him either."

The old G.M. hadn't called him, but he hadn't stopped harassing Lynn, either. The truth was Gabe needed to get down there and deal with the problem, but he couldn't leave yet. Not with his date with Elle coming up. Too much hinged on that. He had to get it right, which meant not ditching her to deal with business. "I'll be down there as soon as possible."

"Which means what, exactly? Today? Tomorrow?"

"I said as soon as possible, and that's what I meant. Give me a few days to tie up a few things here and I'll let you know." As soon as he figured out how to tell Elle he had to leave town. No matter how much he wanted to stay, this needed to be taken care of. *After* their date.

"Fine, Schultz. I'll try to hold him off for a while longer."

"I appreciate it."

"Yeah, yeah, yeah. Talk to you soon." She clicked off.

Gabe hung up and stretched until the bones in his spine popped. Lynn could handle the issue until he made time to get down there. This shouldn't be a huge problem, wouldn't have gotten this far in the first place if he'd stayed in L.A. until things were running smoothly again. It was his responsibility to fix this, one way or another.

Too bad it was the last thing he wanted to do right now.

• • •

"Working late?"

Elle looked up from her desk and smiled at Nathan. "I have a few things I need to take care of, and then I'm heading home."

"Sounds good." He paused in the doorway. "For the record, I'm glad you're not quitting."

"I was never going to quit." She started to reach for a piece of paper to shred, but made her hands still. That he didn't want her to leave, even knowing the truth, settled something deep inside her. "I love the gallery."

"I know you do." He knocked on the doorjamb. "I'll see you tomorrow." Then he was gone, leaving her staring after him.

Elle waited until she heard the outer door shut and lock before she stood. There was nothing here needing to be done that couldn't wait until tomorrow, but she'd wanted some time alone before she went home. It was silly, but this was one of the few places that helped center her when she was feeling out of control.

And she was feeling extremely out of control.

Circling the gallery floor, she finally stopped in front of her favorite painting. Even now, she wasn't sure what it was about the work that drew her so completely, but the first time Elle saw it, she felt like she'd been kicked in the chest. She wanted it with a desire that had been completely unmatched…up until now.

She didn't know what to do about Gabe. Or even if she should do anything at all. Somehow, he'd managed to push his way into her life in a seriously short time and every time she thought about it, she started to get panicky. Because Jason had done the same darn thing. He saw her, he wanted her, and, for all intents and purposes, he'd charmed her panties right off of her. She could still see the mean glint in his eyes when he laughed at her declaration of love, could still feel her heart shattering when he told her how many others girls he'd slept with while they were dating, still ached with the despair that consumed her when he'd turned around and walked away. He was proof that bad boys were bad news.

Gabe looked just like her ex, at least superficially, with his tattoos, rough style, and don't-mess-with-me attitude. But every time fear tried to talk her into backing out of their date she'd remember how he'd taken care of her during her allergic reaction. And the next morning, when he made the top of her head explode and didn't ask for anything in return. She'd given it to him anyway, but she knew to the bottom of her soul that he wouldn't have pushed for more if she hadn't.

No, the more time she spent with Gabe, the more she realized just how much she'd misjudged him. Their time together since the disaster with the sage was more than proof of that.

And, God, the sex was beyond anything she could have imagined.

Elle bit her lip and let her gaze coast over the glorious flowers, their pinks and golds set off by the inkblots beneath them. Beautiful and delicate, but the back beneath them was strong. Even just looking at it straightened her spine and helped steady her resolve.

She wanted this date—a real date—with Gabe, wanted it more than she'd wanted anything since this painting. It didn't matter that her brother would never approve and her mother would go into fits if she knew about it. Elle owed it to herself to get out of her own way and see if these things she felt for him were worth pursuing.

· · ·

Friday night came far too quickly—and not

quickly enough. The days since their time at the lake had dragged on, until it felt like months since she'd seen him last. Elle was ready a full hour before Gabe said he'd pick her up. She paced through the house, adjusting pictures that didn't need to be adjusted, wiping down counters that didn't need to be wiped down, and generally driving herself crazy. When his headlights finally cut through the kitchen windows, Elle was a nervous, bumbling mess.

Unable to pretend she wasn't waiting on pins and needles, she opened the door as he came up the steps. "Hey."

Good lord, he looked fantastic. His jeans were straight-cut and obviously expensive and, combined with the gray dress shirt, had her thoughts diving into the gutter. Elle made an effort to close her mouth and smile at him, even as she fought not to fan herself.

For his part, Gabe seemed just as starstruck as she was. His mouth opened and closed and he swallowed visibly. "You look amazing."

She smoothed down the front of her dress, feeling heat rush to her face. "Thank you. I'm overdressed."

"Don't even think about changing." He held out his hand. "You ready?" The gesture was oddly formal, but it eased some of her anxiety. It was just a date. Sure, a date with a man who made her crazy, but she could do this.

"Yes." Elle paused long enough to lock up, and then they walked to his car. "What's on the agenda?"

He grinned and opened the passenger door. "Wait and see."

"You're teasing me."

"Yep." Gabe bounded around the front of the car and slid into the driver's seat. "Though I have to say—you're doing a damn good job of teasing me."

She blinked. "I'm not doing anything."

"Babe, you're dressed to the nines and grinning at me like I gave you the best present possible just by showing up. If I didn't have an awesome date planned, I'd toss you over my shoulder and take you to bed."

"Oh." She shifted, trying to deal with the surge of desire his words brought. They should shock her—and they did—but they certainly didn't horrify her. "Um…thank you?"

Gabe barked out a laugh. "Anytime. Now let's get out of here before I change my mind."

They drove into town and Elle let herself relax into the comfortable silence. Normally she'd be babbling like an idiot right about now, but the need to do that wasn't there with Gabe. She watched him out of the corner of her eye, wondering when he had become heart-stoppingly gorgeous instead of just a thug. None of this made any sense, but she deliberately chose to let it go. She liked how she felt when she was with him, even after so short a time. Was that really a bad thing just because he didn't match the profile of the imaginary man she'd created? Only time would tell.

She didn't realize their destination until he pulled into the parking lot. "Milford's?"

"A little birdy told me it's your favorite."

Nathan. It had to be. She didn't know why she was so surprised, but a flutter of sheer emotion spiraled through her. Gabe really had done his homework.

Milford's had been around for ages, and was arguably the best seafood place in Spokane. Elle had driven past the building for years before Roxanne took her there for dinner. The menu changed daily, depending on the catch, and she'd never had anything less than fantastic. After half a bottle of wine, she'd once told Roxanne their food was better than sex.

Elle smiled at Gabe as he opened her door.

Yeah, she couldn't make that claim anymore—not after meeting him—but it was still her favorite place to eat, even if she couldn't afford to do it regularly. "Thank you."

"You keep smiling at me like that, and I'll do damn near anything for you." He took her hand, lacing his fingers through hers. "Thank you for coming out with me again. I know the last meal we shared wasn't great."

She barely fought back a shudder at the memory of the bar. "I appreciate the effort."

The inside of Milford's always felt like a step into another world. Everything about the decor screamed money, from the wood paneling to the various art covering the walls. The floors shone as if they'd just been polished and even the lighting created an ambiance of affluence.

They were seated in a secluded corner booth, and she was surprised when Gabe slid next to her instead of taking the seat across the table. He shrugged when he caught her expression. "Can you blame me?"

No, not really. In fact, she had the nearly overwhelming urge to crawl into his lap right here in the middle of the restaurant. His spicy scent wrapped around her, leaving her almost drunk on it. Elle cleared her throat. "I don't know if I'm going to be able to hold a conversation with you so close."

The light in his eyes changed in an instant, going from teasing to straight heat. Gabe cupped her face, his thumbs stroking along her cheekbones. "I like that I affect you like this."

Her breath stuttered in her lungs and her damn nipples perked up. The latter wouldn't be so bad if she was wearing a bra. Sadly, this dress made it impossible. And, of course, Gabe noticed. When his gaze finally moved back to her face, his grin was more satisfied than the cat that ate the canary. He leaned in and pressed a kiss against her lips. Even that brief contact left her shaking. Wanting. She made an involuntary sound of protest when he moved away.

Gabe shook his head. "You're doing a number on my control, babe." He moved to the bench across the table. It didn't help, though, because now she could *see* him. And, from the look on his face, he was doing really, really sexy things to her inside his head.

Her cursed brain was all too helpful in offering up what some of those possibilities could be. Between one breath and the next she was back on her living room couch, naked from the waist down with his mouth on her. If she'd thought the man had wicked lips, it was nothing compared to what he did when he had them on her. If her phone hadn't rung, she would have come hard enough to see stars. Just like he'd promised.

Elle crossed her legs, but it did nothing to help the pulsing heat at her core. In fact, the friction made it worse. She took a hasty drink of water, not sure if she was grateful or annoyed when the waiter approached.

Of course, Gabe didn't seem to have any problem switching from seducer to proper guest. He ordered a beer and then they were both looking at her expectantly. Crap. "Wine, please." When the waiter opened his mouth, she hurried on. "A Cab would be great. Whatever you recommend."

"Very good." The waiter took the wine list. "Have you decided or would you like some more time?"

Gabe's smile was a bit too satisfied. "A few more minutes would be great."

She read over the menu twice before the words actually registered. Good lord, the man was temptation personified. Searching for a distraction, she flipped through the options. Deciding on the salmon, Elle set the menu aside.

Then there was nothing to focus on but Gabe, who seemed all too happy to put all of his attention on her. Elle tried and failed to suppress a shiver. "What are you having?"

"You."

Beneath the heat in his dark eyes, her thoughts tumbled over themselves and then died a silent death. She couldn't move, couldn't speak, could barely breathe. The moment stretched on as her heart tried to beat its way out of her chest.

Gabe reached across the table and took her hand, raising it to brush her knuckles along his cheek. The five o'clock shadow scraped against her skin, leaving her almost unbearably sensitive. He kissed the same spot and then released her. "But not yet."

CHAPTER EIGHTEEN

As Gabe ate, he watched Elle. He couldn't get the image out of his head of taking her on this table, right in the middle of the restaurant. He knew exactly how he'd do it, too—bend her over, push that goddamn tease of a dress up over her hips, and drive into her until she screamed his name.

"What are you thinking?"

From the breathy tone of her voice, she had a decent idea. Which was both a blessing and a curse, since what he really needed right now was to be reeled back in. Instead, she blushed and bit her lip and, damn it, he could still see her nipples through the dress's thin fabric.

Gabe took a long drink of his beer before answering, searching for a way to tone down the sexual tension they had going ever since they'd spent the day in bed together. In the days since, he kept catching himself daydreaming about being inside her, about *making love*. It was a term he'd spent years laughing at. How was he supposed to know how apt—how goddamn addicting—it was? But he couldn't afford to let it distract him. Tonight was going to be perfect, even if he had to walk around with blue balls for the entirety of it.

"Just thinking about this tattoo I'm putting together for a friend."

Interest lit her features. "What's it of?"

"Well, that's the difficult part. He wants to bring in a few different elements, and I haven't figured out a way to make it work." When she leaned forward, propping her chin in her hands, Gabe decided he might as well keep going. It wasn't often he had a captive audience to bounce ideas off of. "You see, it's like this—he has this thing for Norse mythology and wants to bring in a couple different aspects of Odin."

"Why Norse?"

"Paul teaches a whole series of mythology and religion courses over at one of the local colleges. He based his entire thesis on Norse myths— though don't ask me to explain the details."

"A college professor with a thing for tattoos." Elle shook her head, her lips pulling up into a smile. "The world keeps getting stranger."

"I guess." He took a bite and chewed slowly. "There are a lot of people out there who come in for tats just because they can. Because it's the trendy thing to do. But then you have the people who are true...I don't even know what word to use. For some people, they're almost like a religious experience. For others, like Paul, they're a visual marking of one of life's milestones. He gets tattoos because he loves them, and because each one has a story and a history." Shit, he hadn't meant to preach at her.

But Elle wasn't searching for the nearest exit. She watched him raptly, her meal apparently forgotten. "My mother thinks they're all trashy. Obviously, our opinions differ on that score."

He had a feeling their opinions differed on a lot of things. Thank God. "Tats aren't for everyone. But they also aren't as cut-and-dried as a lot of people think."

"What about yours? Do they each have a story?"

"Most of them." He shrugged when her eyebrows rose. "I'm not going to pretend this was a deep and meaningful choice." Gabe pointed to his shoulder.

Elle closed her eyes for a brief moment. "The…odd skull?"

Of course she wouldn't recognize the Misfits emblem. They really were from different worlds. "Yeah. It was my first. My favorite band at the time."

"Doesn't that, by definition, mean something to you?"

She had a point. "Yeah, but I literally went into a shop, sat down, and told the guy this is what I wanted. There wasn't a whole lot of thought that went into it."

"What about the other ones?" She motioned to his chest and arm.

"The bio-mech stuff?" Gabe rubbed his shoulder. "Ever since I restored my Camaro, I've been fascinated by how things are put together. I build little things, and I've been toying with plans for a true mech suit. You saw *Avatar*?"

Elle smiled. "I liked it a lot."

"Me too. You know those suits the soldiers fought in?" He waited for her to nod. "Something like that. It's a geeky hobby, and not something I talk about to most people. I haven't had time to play with it lately."

"So that relates to your tattoo…"

"Well, while doing research for these machines, I got distracted with how the human body is put together, and how it would look if it were part machine. From there it was only natural to translate my hobby into a tattoo."

"It's gorgeous." She fiddled with her wineglass. "Will you tell me about your arm now? The real meaning behind it?"

So she'd seen through his shield the first time he talked about it. Good. He didn't make a habit of sharing the meaning behind that particular tat, though. Only Nathan and his mentor knew the full story. Still, Elle already knew about his mother. It wasn't much of a leap to tell her this and he found he *wanted* to. She obviously appreciated the significance, and he wanted to share this with her. "The verses are a compilation of my mother's favorites."

He pointed to each, having memorized the words long ago because of how often his mother repeated them. "Hosea 11:9. She used that one a lot to remind us of what we're supposed to aspire to be. The context was off, but Mom never seemed to care.

"Micah 7:7." Gabe had to stop for a second and clear his throat. "She prayed every day for our lives to get better, spent a good hour on her knees before she tucked us into bed, and she never once lost hope."

He glanced at Elle and found her watching him closely. "Joshua 1:5. 'I will never leave you nor forsake you.' Mom looked at that the same way she looked on the rest, but this one was as much a promise to me and Nathan as it was to her. She could have taken off, left us with my dad and gotten out. She didn't.

"Revelations 21:4. That…that one is pretty self explanatory."

Gabe tensed, half expecting pity, but she only smiled and traced the edge of the tattoo with her fingertips. "It's beautiful."

"Thank you." He found himself smiling back, the ache he normally felt regarding his past lessening, just a little.

Elle sat back and sipped her wine. "You're very passionate about tattoos."

"They're my thing. Nathan's got his art, I have my shop."

She leaned back and sipped her wine. "I thought your thing was the nightclubs. You have, what, five now?"

"Someone's been checking up on me."

A blush stained her cheeks a really cute pink. "I was curious."

"No, they aren't my thing. I enjoy running the business and the rush of opening a new club. There's nothing like it in the world, but my tattoo shop is my home."

It was something he'd never said out loud because it sounded so lame, but Elle didn't laugh at him. Instead, understanding lit her blue eyes. "That's how Nathan is with his main gallery."

"We each have our own things." He really didn't want to talk about Nathan right now. "So, what about you? What's your passion? Your pipe dream?"

She fidgeted. "I don't know."

"Bullshit. Excuse my French." Someone as grounded as Elle knew exactly what her pipe dream was, even if she obviously didn't want to admit it. Curiosity pricked him. What was it? It had to be something good if she didn't want to admit it out loud.

"That's not really French."

"You're avoiding. Tell me." As her face turned even redder, he realized what it must be. "Your painting."

"It's stupid." Elle ran a finger around the tip of her wineglass.

"Doesn't sound stupid." He took a drink of his beer. "So do it."

"It's not that easy."

"Again, I say bullshit." When she slanted a sharp glance his way, he shrugged. "I'm not saying you're going to reach Nathan status overnight, but why not pursue it?"

"Oh, I don't know. Because it's a foolish career with no dependable income? The starving artist thing is highly overrated."

Her bouts of bitchiness were really starting to grow on him, which just proved how in over his head he was. "That's your mother speaking. Besides, what's stopping you from doing it in your spare time?"

Elle frowned. "You're being annoyingly logical right now."

"I do that sometimes. One of my many charms." Gabe finished his beer. As much as he didn't want to steer the conversation in this direction, it had to be done. "Have you told Nathan?"

"God, no."

"Why not?"

"Because..." She made some obscure hand motion that meant exactly nothing. "I can't."

"Yeah, that wasn't even close to a decent reason."

"You don't understand. He's like a god within

the artist circles—the man can do no wrong. And his sculptures are beyond description. Compared to him, I might as well be finger-painting."

"There's your first problem, babe. You shouldn't be comparing yourself to anyone but you."

"That's not even a little realistic." She sighed. "I'm sorry. It's just that the idea of going to Nathan and telling him my dream is to own a gallery filled with my paintings… No way. He'll laugh at me."

"You obviously don't know my brother as well as you think you do." Nathan would never laugh at an aspiring artist, let alone one he actually cared about as a friend. And even if he *was* asshole enough to laugh at her, Gabe would punch his pretty face in.

Either way, it was a moot point.

"I guess."

Okay, definitely time to change the subject. Again. Apparently the waiter thought so too, because he showed up, check in hand. "I hope you enjoyed your meal."

"It was fantastic." He waited for the man to leave before he dropped the appropriate amount of cash on the table and scooted out of the booth. Elle beat him to her feet, giving him an eyeful of her back. The dress crisscrossed a couple times, its black startling against her barely tanned skin. Gabe wanted to run his fingers under those straps until she was shaking.

It would have to wait, though. He had other plans for the rest of the night.

As they walked through the front door, he slipped an arm around her waist. Instantly, she melted against him. He could really get used to this, to these casual touches, the comfort of being able to hold her without it being solely about sex. The sex was great, but the years had left him starved for these small things that so many people took for granted. They strolled down the sidewalk, some of the tension evaporating.

"Are you going to tell me where we're going?"

"You up for a walk?"

She laughed. "You're really running with this whole secret thing. Sure, I'm up for a walk."

"Good." He turned them at the corner, heading for the bridge. "So tell me about your brother. Are you close?"

"We used to be close." She shrugged. "But after...well, something happened in college, and now there's this distance between us that was never there before. It doesn't help that he's in

Japan right now and it's hard to line up the time differences."

"I'm sorry." He couldn't imagine anything that could drive him and Nathan apart. Then again, if his little brother had tried for Elle, it might have been enough to bring them to blows. It wasn't a comfortable thought.

"So am I. I mean, I understand he's overprotective of me. I'm his little sister. But there have to be boundaries."

There was only one thing proven to drive overprotective brothers off their rocker—their sister dating someone they didn't approve of. Someone like Gabe. "Who was he?"

Elle jumped. "Who was who?"

Oh yeah, like that innocent tone would work on him. "Who was the guy your brother hated?"

She tried to pull away, but he kept her easily at his side. "I don't want to talk about it."

"Babe…"

"Oh lord, fine. It's not a big deal. We dated a while. I thought I was in love. He wasn't. He cheated on me and then dumped me in front of all our friends. Ian went ballistic. The end." There was only the slightest quiver in the words to let him know how much it still hurt her.

Gabe decided he and Elle's older brother

might just get along. "What's this guy's name?" He knew people who knew people—and that was if he didn't take care of the little shit himself.

"No. Absolutely not. It's ancient history."

"There's no such thing, babe."

Elle stopped and turned to face him. "I don't need you or my big brother to fight my battles for me. And I certainly don't need you to go around bashing in the heads of people who hurt me. It's barbaric."

"Maybe you need some barbarian in your life."

CHAPTER NINETEEN

It was so strange to be walking through downtown at night on the arm of a guy who, not three weeks ago, Elle would have crossed the street to avoid. And, yeah, she hadn't been too thrilled with the way he pushed her with both the art stuff and her ex-boyfriend, but the night was still going far better than she'd expected.

"Do you like to dance?"

A thrill of foreboding snaked through her. "That depends on a number of things." The first being how much she'd had to drink. Even now, with a single glass of wine under her belt, a delicious warmth spread through her body.

"I bet." Gabe's fingers dipped beneath the edge of the back of her dress. It was a relatively innocent touch, but it set her skin on fire. "We're almost there."

Even this early on Friday night, there were quite a few people out and about, all taking advantage of the nice weather. Most were dressed in casual clothes, which would have made her feel out of place if she had the space in her head for such thoughts. As it was, Elle's entire being focused on the tiny circles Gabe traced over her skin.

She wanted him naked and back in her bed. Heck, she'd been completely preoccupied with reliving the memories of their lovemaking for the last couple of days. Especially after he'd gotten her so close on the beach, right there where anyone could have seen what he was doing to her. The very thought made her blush, even as she wanted it again. If Gabe hadn't been so into making this night perfect for her, she would have dragged him home so he could have her for dessert.

When he withdrew, she had to actually bite back a sound of protest. They'd stopped in front of a nondescript door on a tall brick building with no windows. There was a vertical sign reading Ascension, but otherwise it was completely without decoration.

"I'd like you to see my business." Gabe took

her hand and they walked through the door, nodding at the hulking man standing just inside. Holy crap, that guy was *huge*. Elle didn't get much more than a glimpse of a bald head and forbidding expression before she was swept along into a large room.

Whatever she expected, it wasn't this. It was like she'd stepped into another Milford's, only this one had a huge bar stretching from one wall to the other down the right side of the room. The rest of the space was occupied with three pool tables and a scattering of round tables and chairs. People in business attire gathered in small groups, talking softly while some song she'd never heard before played over the speakers. "Oh, wow."

"Not what you expected?"

"You know it isn't."

Gabe grinned. "Don't act too relieved. There's more."

More? She followed him back the way they'd come to where a staircase and elevator had been hidden in a small corridor. "I don't understand."

"Have you ever been to the club Dublin?" When she shook her head, he continued. "Well, they have clubs in other cities with the same concept. Five floors, each with a different theme. This is the entrance level—kind of chill right now, but after ten we switch the music as the younger crowd starts showing up. Then, if you want quiet, you go to the top."

She had to admit, it was a fascinating idea. Elle wasn't much of a clubgoer, but she could see the appeal of having several flavors of music and crowds to choose from without having to switch buildings or pay an extra cover charge.

"What's your poison? Techno, hip-hop, or country?"

Though there was the temptation to see them all, she went with the one least likely to traumatize her. "Country."

Gabe stepped into the elevator and pressed four. "Can you swing dance?"

Yes, but she was surprised he'd think to ask. "I haven't tried since high school. Can you?"

"I had a friend who was into that sort of thing. Can't do the lifts, but I can spin you around the floor a time or two." He grinned. "You up for it?"

That expression did funny things to her stomach. Despite her best effort, Elle ended up grinning right back at him. "Sure."

The country floor was both what she expected and completely different. There were the typical trappings found in this type of bar everywhere, but everything was of a really high quality. Though the bar itself looked like several barn doors attached together. When she leaned against it, she found it'd been sanded down to an almost silky smoothness. The majority of the room was occupied by a huge dance floor and stage, which seemed to indicate they had live music from time to time. That left the other half of the room, with the square bar immediately next to the elevator and a handful of tables and chairs on the other side.

Already, the music was going and the place was half-full. Almost everyone was under thirty, but there was a group of older men and women swinging around the dance floor.

"Those are our regulars." Elle jolted when Gabe spoke in her ear. "They come out after dinner, dance for a while, and then go home before the heavy crowds hit."

A man flipped his partner around, pulling off a move Elle hadn't seen outside of competitions. Dang. "Sounds like fun."

"Would you like a drink?"

She didn't want to get wasted, but maybe one drink would be okay? Elle didn't know. It was hard to think with the length of his body pressed against hers. "A lemon drop if they can make it."

"Babe, this is my club. Of course they can make it." He caught her earlobe with his teeth, pressing just hard enough to send a shiver racking her body. Then Gabe was gone, strolling to the bar as if he didn't have a care in the world.

In an effort to keep from watching him like some love-struck teenager, Elle made her way to one of the tables. Here, she had a great view of the dance floor. The more she watched, the harder it was to ignore the desire to move. Sure, she couldn't match them for skill, but memories came over her in waves, all of them highlighting the fun she'd had with friends back in high school.

By the time Gabe slid into the chair next to her, she was determined to try. Then his thigh pressed against hers and his hand dropped to her knee, right where the hem of her dress rested, and she forgot everything but him. Elle took her drink with fumbling fingers and sipped it. Lemon tartness exploded on her tongue, lending to the warmth already circulating through her body. He leaned in, close enough to give that kiss she was so preoccupied with. Elle watched his lips move, already feeling them on her body. "Want to dance?"

Dancing was good. Dancing meant she wasn't going to throw herself at him in the middle of this club. Elle nodded. They moved onto the floor, Gabe expertly leading her through the other dancers. He spun her out and then into his arms, surprisingly light on his feet, and the moves came back as if she'd never forgotten them.

The world narrowed down to the feel of Gabe's hands on her body, the beat of the music, the sweat on her skin. One song blended into another and they kept right on dancing, even as the crowd around them faded into a younger set. Finally, breathless, she shook her head. "Break. I need a break."

Gabe led the way back to their table. When Elle collapsed in her seat, she gave her drink a suspicious look. "I think I'm good."

"Babe, no one touched your drink."

"You don't know that."

"Actually I do." He nodded at the bartender. "She watched them."

"She's all the way across the room. How the heck would she know?"

"You are so damn cute when you're being paranoid." He hooked the back of her neck and pulled her in, crushing his lips against hers.

Elle opened her mouth without having any intention of doing so. She ran her fingers through his hair as his tongue traced hers. God, he tasted amazing. Elle stroked her hands down his chest and back up again to cup his face.

Gabe shifted back and she almost yelped when he lifted her into his lap. But then his tongue tangled with hers, washing her away on a tide of desire. It beat beneath her skin, demanding things she very much wanted to follow through on after experiencing them firsthand the other day. Gabe's fingers slipped beneath her dress, barely an inch above her knee, but it was as if he'd stroked directly over her core. Her fingers dug into his shoulders as she shivered.

When he nipped her bottom lip, she moaned. There was no way he could have heard the sound—not with the music as loud as it was—but Gabe pulled away, his eyes gone dark with passion. "Come with me."

"Okay." No hesitation. No questions. Right now, with her body still shaking from his touch, she'd go anywhere he asked.

He moved through the crowd, so fast it was almost a struggle to keep up. If it weren't for his hand nearly crushing hers, she would have lost him in an instant. She thought they were headed for the elevator, but Gabe swerved around a couple making out and stopped in front of the bar. He flipped up a section of it and closed it behind them. Before she could ask what the heck they were doing, he dragged her through a door.

There was a short hallway with two more doors. One was obviously a freezer and the other, which was apparently their destination, was a storage room.

CHAPTER TWENTY

If Gabe didn't have her right this second, he was going to lose his damn mind. He pulled Elle into his arms, kissing her again. How kissing alone could make him so insane was a mystery, but with Elle, he could do it for hours. For her part, she didn't shove him off and call him a Neanderthal again. Instead, she melted under his hands, molding herself to his chest. Christ, the scent of the woman was enough to drive him wild.

He pulled back to say, "I've tried so hard to be good, but fuck, I need you."

"Yes."

That simple word. No more. But it was enough. Gabe turned until her back was to the door and kissed his way down her neck, tugging her dress along with him. He'd known she wasn't wearing a bra, but he still groaned when the fabric fell to reveal her breasts. Even in the dim shadows, they were something. Perfcct. Absolutely perfect.

Though desperation tugged at him, getting worse with each passing second, he took his time. Some things couldn't be rushed, and this woman deserved to be worshipped. He cupped her breasts, using his thumbs to circle her nipples. Elle's groan was loud enough to be heard over the barely muted music.

It was too much. He couldn't wait.

Releasing her breasts, he dropped to his knees and slid his hands up her legs, lifting her dress until her panties were revealed. Gabc balled the fabric in one hand and used the other to yank down the lace.

"What—" Her breath hissed out when he licked up her center. Christ, she tasted even better than he remembered.

It wasn't enough, not in this position. He shoved her dress into her hands. "Hang on to this." Before Elle could respond, Gabe used his hold on the back of her thighs to lift and spread them, bracing her against the wall. It left her completely helpless and open beneath his tongue. He took his time, tasting every inch of her before he zeroed in on her clit, light flicks causing her to shake so hard he almost lost his grip. Elle grasped his hair, holding him in place. As if he'd want to be anywhere else.

"Please don't stop."

Like hell he was going to stop. Gabe sucked on her clit, needing to feel her come against his face again. Her moans drove him on, but he didn't give in to the urge to hurry. When her hips started rolling to meet him, he matched the pace, keeping it steady even as she gasped and thrashed. Then her body went tight, her nails digging into his scalp. He welcomed the pain, keeping up gentle licks until she stopped shuddering.

Lowering her to the floor, Gabe waited until she locked her knees before he stood. Elle was already reaching for his pants, and he didn't need any further encouragement. He didn't expect her to drop to her knees, though.

"Babe—" At the first tentative swipe of her tongue, his mind went blank. Gabe could only stare down at her as she wrapped her lips around his cock. There were no words to describe this. He couldn't…

Elle took him deeper and his back hit the wall. Her tongue stroked the underside of his length even as the head of his cock bumped the back of her throat. Christ, at this rate, his knees were going to give out. Her mouth felt so goddamn good, but it was more than that. Having *Elle* on her knees and obviously enjoying herself… Never in a million years would he have expected it. Not here. Not like this. But, God, he loved every second of it. She made a humming noise as she cupped his balls, and the sensation of her nails lightly dragging over his delicate skin had pressure building in the base of his cock.

No, it was too soon. Gabe needed to be inside her. He laced his fingers loosely through her hair, tugging gently until she stood. A quick glance around didn't give him any good options—he refused to take her on the floor. The shelves wouldn't hold them, either. Christ, this was a stupid place to do this.

"Turn around." He took her hands and braced them on the door and then cupped her breasts, playing with her nipples until she arched against him. Keeping hold of her left breast, he lifted her dress again and nudged her legs further apart. His cock nestled right up against her ass and when she pushed back against him, he almost lost it right there. "Fuck, Elle. I need to find a condom."

He went for his wallet, but she grabbed his hand and shook her head. "We're covered. Now, Gabe. Please."

He pressed against her entrance and then he was inside, the sensation of taking Elle without a condom more potent than he expected. The sheer amount of trust she must have had in him to allow it, not to mention her lack of hesitation, staggered him on such a profound level that he had to take a moment to gather himself. He would do right by her. He'd never give her reason to regret trusting him this much.

Gabe kept his strokes shallow, working his way a little deeper with each one. Already, Elle's body was shaking. He started to ask if she was okay, but then she shoved back against him and all he could do was groan.

"More, Gabe. I need more."

This wasn't what he'd intended. Gabe wanted to take her slow, make her crazy for him, but her urgency was like a drug to his system. Using his grip on her hips, he pounded into her, the force of the motion slapping their skin together in a sound Gabe could hear even over the music in the other room.

Shit, shit, shit. Too much. He'd gone too far.

When Elle pulled forward, he almost let her

go, but then she slammed back onto his cock. She moaned, moving forward again, and Gabe took the hint. Getting a better grip on her hips, he gave into the need demanding he drive into her. They met each other, stroke for stroke, as heat built at the base of Gabe's spine. Still thrusting, he leaned forward, kissing the back of her neck as he slid his hand between her legs and pressed against her clit. With each stroke, she rubbed against his hand, her moans growing louder.

"Come for me, babe."

She went wild, her orgasm rippling around his cock until he completely lost control. Pumping into her, Gabe came so hard his knees actually buckled. He caught himself on the door and tried to relearn how to breathe. Too much. Not enough. Never enough. He wasn't sure he was prepared to ever let Elle go.

• • •

The door vibrated against Elle's cheek and she jumped, smacking Gabe in the face with the back of her head. "Oh God, someone's at the door."

He groaned and let her off the wall, and when she turned around he looked really damn pleased with himself. "Babe, that was fantastic. I don't even know if I can walk right now."

That made two of them.

She pulled her dress up, fumbling with the straps. Whoever was on the other side apparently wasn't giving up. Instead, they knocked harder. "Gabe, they're going to come in here."

"Relax. It's all good."

It didn't feel all good. Okay, that wasn't really true. Her body felt great—over-the-top mind-blowing sex could do that to a girl—but her mind was awhirl with what they'd just done. Unprotected sex in a freaking storage closet. She was on the Pill, sure, but either Elle had lost her mind or Gabe meant more to her than she anticipated.

That was an alarming thought.

Gabe kissed her, and Elle's worries faded. Sure, this hadn't exactly been her classiest moment, but it didn't matter. She cared about Gabe and he obviously cared about her. That meant something, even if they weren't exactly following the traditional path.

Note to self: never, ever, under any circumstances, tell Ian about this. He'd lose his freaking mind. And she so wasn't even thinking about her mother's reaction right now.

Once her dress was in place, she looked

around. "Uh, where is my underwear?"

"Don't know, babe." The pounding got even more intense and the doorknob rattled. "But we gotta get out of here."

"I can't leave without my panties."

"I own this joint. No one is going to mess with them, okay? Trust me."

Oh God, he wasn't joking. It didn't look like she was going to have a choice. Elle sighed—at least there was no way he could hear the faint sound—and finally nodded. "Okay."

Gabe took her hand and, with one last grin, opened the door. Whoever she expected on the other side, it wasn't the huge bald guy from the front door. "We got a problem, boss."

Instantly, all joking was gone from his face. "What kind of problem?"

The giant shot a look at her and raised his eyebrows. "The, ah, important kind."

Oh, great. That was subtle. Obviously he didn't want to say anything in front of her. Elle rolled her eyes, and tried not to let it sting when Gabe didn't immediately jump to her defense. It was just business. It didn't mean he was keeping secrets. She was feeling off because of what just happened. Right.

She searched for something to say. "I'll

just grab another drink while you take care of this." After the sex, her throat was parched. Because, really, she wasn't running away because she wasn't ready to deal with the shift in the relationship.

"You sure, babe?"

She might be a lot of things, but clingy wasn't one of them. And Elle would never want to get in the way of his business...whatever it was. "Sure." Even if it didn't make her completely comfortable, it wasn't like she could demand an explanation right here and now. It was his club so, technically, it wasn't her business.

"I'll be right back. You won't even know I'm gone." He kissed her again, pulling Elle against his body. Despite her best efforts, she melted into him. It was only the bouncer clearing his throat that tore them apart. As Gabe walked away, Elle took a slow, shaky breath. Sex in closets. Making out in public. It was like she was a stranger.

She didn't know how she felt about it. Though she did know what Roxanne would say—jump back in that closet for another round. And she knew what Gabe would say—babe, you're overthinking again. It was like having two devils on her shoulder, except one was her best friend and the other the man responsible for the best sex of her life.

Okay, that metaphor just took a turn for the weird.

With a mental shrug, she headed toward the busy bar. It would be a bit of a wait, but she didn't mind. Elle needed time to center herself. The crowd pressed in on her, conflicting smells of too many perfumes and colognes assaulting her senses. Good Lord, did everyone shower in the stuff before they came out? It was enough to make her wonder if she'd be better off on a different floor. But she couldn't do that. Elle didn't even know if Gabe had his phone—they'd spend the rest of the night trying to find each other.

Before she could make a decision, a gap appeared in front of her and Elle slid into it. She signaled the bartender, but still had to wait five minutes for the woman to make her way over. "What's up?"

"Can I get a…" Not a lemon drop—there was no way she could get through this crowd without spilling every drop from the martini glass. "A vodka tonic."

"Sure thing. On boss man's tab?"

"Yes, please." She'd pay him back later. Or just, heck, let him pay for her freaking drink.

Why was she even worrying about this? Her thoughts were on overdrive, tumbling over each other in their effort to bring her fears right to the forefront.

Elle sipped her drink and nearly spat it back out. Holy crap, that was nasty. Served her right for ordering something without having tried it first. But, heck, plenty of people drank this. At least, Roxanne did. Guess it just wasn't Elle's thing. With a sigh, she set the tumbler on the bar and turned to watch the people moving through the room. They were mostly the college crowd, all young and dressed in a variety of clothes, none that had much to do with country music as far as she could tell.

Despite the good music and people-watching, it didn't take long for her to get bored. Where was Gabe? He should have been back by now. She pulled out her phone and glanced at it. Fifteen freaking minutes? Criminy. She was done waiting on him.

Elle pushed off the bar and headed for the elevator. The music she'd enjoyed before now grated on her nerves. She punched a button at random and tapped her foot as it descended. The doors opened and music pounded through her body, so loud she couldn't manage to string two thoughts together. From her vantage point, Elle could see how people were crammed in from one wall to the other, shimmying in an almost-orgy while some rapper went on about the backseat of his car.

No way could she find any single person in there. Elle smacked the next number down, wondering if maybe she should just wait by the front door. Eventually Gabe was bound to finish with his business, whatever it was, and come looking for her. When he didn't find her on the country floor, he'd try to find her.

Wouldn't he?

This time when the doors opened, it was techno blasting through the space. Even though this room was slightly less crowded than the other, the dancing was just as suggestive and the music…cripes, she didn't even hear words.

Elle was so out of her element it wasn't even funny.

There were only two options left—the main floor or the top one. Crossing her fingers, she pressed the number five and hoped for the best. At least there was no one in the elevator to witness her spiral into self-doubt. Or, worse, trying to chat her up.

At least this time when the doors opened,

there was only the faint sound of classical music and a soft murmur of voices. Finally, something she could relate to. Even if Gabe wasn't here, she could actually ask someone where the best place was to find him.

Plan in place, Elle marched over to the bar. The man behind it was either in his early forties or one of those guys whose hair went silver early. After taking in his unlined face, she decided it was probably the latter. He gave her a winning smile that had to earn him a lot of tips. "What can I get you?"

The very last thing she needed right now was alcohol. "I'm looking for Gabe Schultz. We were on the country floor and the bouncer said they had a problem he needed to take care of." Crap, what if she wasn't supposed to tell him that?

The guy didn't look surprised. In fact, his smile never even flickered. "Offices are on the first floor. Not sure if that's where he'd be but, as you can see, he's not up here."

Seemed easy enough, and she was smart enough to recognize a dismissal when she heard it. Obviously this guy wanted nothing to do with her as soon as he pegged her as a nonpaying customer. "Thanks."

She waited for the elevator, suddenly

exhausted. After all the excitement and chaos, she just wanted to go home and crawl into bed. If she got to do it in Gabe's arms, then all the better for it.

The street-level bar was quieter than the rest, but maybe that was just by comparison. Aside from the handful of people around the pool tables, everyone was sitting and drinking. She looked around, wondering where the offices were situated. Since she hadn't seen any possibilities of hallways or doors while walking in, they had to be in the back.

Elle wove through the tables, walking parallel to the bar. Sure enough, there was a hallway tucked into the back corner of the room. She followed it, noting the restrooms just around the corner, and kept going. The offices had to be back here somewhere. As she turned another corner, she caught the murmur of voices—a woman and a man.

That wasn't Gabe…right?

Walking slower, she strained to hear what was being said, but it was no use. There was only the tone. She couldn't catch a single word. Finally, Elle gave up and pressed her ear to the door, ignoring the guilt of eavesdropping.

A woman laughed. "Oh, sweet cheeks, you

have no idea."

"I'm sure I do. I've been around the block a few times. This is nothing new."

There was no mistaking the amusement in Gabe's voice. Elle's heart gave a half beat and took up residence somewhere south of her right ankle. Surely he didn't mean what it sounded like?

"I bet you say that to all the girls."

"Only the pretty ones. I can't believe you flew up here."

"How else was I supposed to get you back to L.A.? Because all my phone calls obviously weren't cutting it."

All her phone calls? Oh God, he'd been on the phone with this woman *while he was in Elle's house.*

"I know you were having a hard time and I'm sorry for taking so long with stuff up here. As soon as I get back down to California, we'll figure this all out."

Wait, what? He was going back to L.A.? And he hadn't told her? Not to mention the woman he was going with.

"I'm just glad you'll be back."

Elle's breath tore through her lungs. Surely this was a mistake. She was misinterpreting what they were saying. She had to be. Panic welled, so thick in her throat she could barely breathe past it. The door was heavier than she expected—which probably accounted for the muted voices—but she got it open enough to slip into the room.

The sight that met her stopped her in her tracks.

Gabe stood close to a tall, purple-haired woman. Too close. At the sound of the door, he turned to face Elle, wiping his mouth. The world went white around the edges, the entire room spinning slowly before slamming into focus. There was no mistaking the lipstick smeared across the back of his hand, or the conversation he just had.

In a rush, all of Elle's fears swarmed her, each demanding their due. In a flash, she was nineteen again and standing in the middle of a group of her friends. Jason had his arm around a new girl, despite the fact he'd taken her virginity less than forty-eight hours ago. Her heart thudded in her chest as his grin turned vicious. "What? Did you think I'd ever be satisfied with a frigid bitch like you? About as sexy as fucking a corpse." And then he'd turned and walked away, laughing at her the entire time.

Not again. Never again. She'd been so sure Gabe wasn't a lying, cheating bastard after their week together, but apparently her first impression had been right. They just had sex and he was already kissing some other woman and making plans to jet off to California. Oh my God, he'd played her for a fool. Not only that—he'd brought her down to his level.

Her mother had been right all along.

"You…" So many words crowded forward, she couldn't get more than the single one out.

Gabe leaped away from the woman, as if she'd caught fire. It was far too late for that, though. Elle had already seen the truth. Distantly, she noticed how beautiful the woman was in her designer clothes and edgy purple hair. Just the kind of woman Gabe would really want, the kind who understood the game better than Elle ever would.

The room blurred and swirled around the edges. She had to get out of here. Right now. Because next he'd say he could explain and, if she sat around long enough, she'd probably believe him. Because, God, hadn't he talked right over every single one of her fears, lulling her into believing he actually cared? In the face of everything that happened tonight, the very idea was laughable.

Gabe crept toward her, hands out like she was a skittish horse. He should know better. "Elle? Babe, breathe."

She shook her head. He'd lied to her then, and he'd lie to her again if she gave him half a chance. And, chump that she was, she'd fallen for it. Guess she really hadn't learned from her mistakes with Jason.

Well, darn it, she was going to learn from them now.

The resolution calmed her frantic breathing. She backed up, holding up a hand when he made as if to follow. "Look, you're obviously busy here, so I'll just leave you to it."

"No. Goddamn it, Elle!"

The damn door was nearly her undoing. As Elle fought it open, she could feel Gabe walking toward her as if they were bound by some freakish connection. But that was crap. There was nothing connecting them but a string of bad decisions.

She should have kept her damn panties on. Finally, the door opened enough for her to slide through. She thought she heard Gabe yell her name, but Elle didn't stick around to find out. Tears blurred her vision and her entire focus narrowed down to getting the heck out of this stupid club and getting herself home. She'd been a damn fool to show up in the first place.

Choking back a sob, she burst onto the street, nearly tripping over her own feet in the process.

A sudden, completely irrational urge to call her brother arose. Before she could talk herself out of it, she pulled out her phone and flipped through the contacts. It was only when she pressed the phone to her ear that she paused to wonder what time it was in Japan right now. Before she could change her mind and hang up, Ian answered, "Hey, Ellie."

She sniffed, trying to get control of her emotions. "Hey."

"What's wrong?"

Elle shook her head, wiping at her eyes, but the tears wouldn't stop. Now that she had him on the line, she didn't know what to say.

All the warmth disappeared from his voice. "Tell me what happened. Now."

This was a mistake. She should have known better than to call Ian, especially when she couldn't stop crying, but there was no help for it now. If she hung up on him, he'd be on the next plane home. A little thing like going AWOL would mean nothing to her brother if he thought his little sister in trouble.

"Who is he?"

Of course he'd pick up on the fact this was about a guy. Her brother was too smart by half. Elle swallowed, wishing she had a tissue to blow her nose. "It's not a big deal. I'm sorry I bothered you with this."

"Ellie." Ian sighed, some of the stone-cold-killer leaching out of his tone, replaced by the brother who'd wiped her tears when she dumped her bike and skinned her knee. "Please tell me what happened."

She sniffed again. "I…I think I made a mess of things." The tears started up again, worse this time. "I really l-liked this guy, a-and it's ruined. Everything's r-ruined."

"What guy? Your boss?"

"N-no." The enormity of the last two weeks cascaded down around her shoulders. Not only did she try—and fail—to seduce Nathan, she'd slept with his brother. Then…then she went and lost her idiot head and actually started to fall for him when all he wanted from her was sex to take the edge off before he could get back to L.A. and another woman. Elle pressed her hand to her mouth, trying to stifle the sob threatening to emerge. "I d-don't know w-what to do."

"You can't go to Mom and Dad's like this. Mom will freak out. Are you still friends with that woman—Roxanne or whatever her name is?"

"Yes."

"Call her. Either get a cab or have her come pick you up, but don't drive tonight, okay?"

"Okay," she whispered. Just like always, Ian's take-charge attitude centered her, even if it didn't quite counteract what she'd just done. If he knew… No, she couldn't tell Ian. He'd kill Gabe.

"Do you want me to call her? Or, shit, is there anything I can do but sit here and listen to you cry on the phone? Not being able to help you is killing me, Ellie."

She wouldn't be able to hold back this sob forever—Elle had to get him off the phone before she gave it voice. "Can I call you tomorrow, when I'm…you know?"

"Yeah." He sighed. "Do that. I'll be home in a few weeks—everything will be better then."

Everything would be better and nothing would be better. Having Ian around wasn't going to change how things had blown up in her face with Gabe. "I'll talk to you later. Love you."

"Love you, too."

Picking a direction at random, she started

walking. Once she calmed down, she'd find a place and call a cab. Except the idea of riding home alone in the back of one nearly sent her to her knees. Without her brother's calming presence, her sobs came so fast now they were nearly one long keen of despair. Elle wrapped her arms around herself, wanting her brother, wanting her friend, wanting to go home, basically wanting a freaking time machine to take her back two weeks so she could beat herself over the back of the head for ever thinking that climbing into bed with Nathan was a good idea. It wasn't a good idea. It was the worst freaking idea she ever had, and it'd sent her into an unmatched downward spiral.

She didn't even recognize herself anymore.

Chapter Twenty-One

What the fuck was wrong with that woman? She came bursting into the room, took one look at him, and hightailed it out of here, obviously hell-bent on thinking the worst of the situation. She'd been so horrified to see him wiping lipstick off his face, she hadn't waited around for an explanation.

Lynn hadn't kissed him, not like that. She'd just done her usual kiss-on-each-cheek and Elle had opened the door before he'd had the chance to wipe off the smudge of her damned lipstick he could still feel mucking up his face.

By the time Gabe hit the street, Elle was long gone and not answering her phone. He got to his car in record time and practically flew to her house, but the lights were off and obviously no one was home.

Shit, what if she was in trouble? Spokane wasn't exactly the crappiest place in the world, but bad things did happen from time to time. A woman walking alone at night could be more than enough to get the predators sniffing around. Especially if she was as pretty as Elle.

Goddamn it. If she hadn't run off like that, they wouldn't be in this situation to begin with. He dialed without looking and held the phone to his ear. After three rings, Nathan picked up. "What's going on?"

No point in going into how many ways the night had gone from fantastic to fucked up. "There was a misunderstanding and Elle took off. I can't find her."

"You sure she didn't go home?"

"I just checked her house, and her phone is going straight to voice mail. Last I saw her, she was practically running away from the club." From him. Again. Christ, this was becoming a habit he could do without. He'd thought they were beyond the snap judgments and her hoity-toity attitude. Apparently it was something they'd never get past. "Where would she go?"

"Her brother is deployed right now, so my guess would be either Roxanne's or her parents."

Gabe thought fast. Elle would be a mess.

Between the sex and the date itself, he didn't see her being able to face her parents, especially not this late at night. "Do you have her friend's number?"

"Let me see." There was the faint sound of his brother tapping through his phone and then Nathan was back. He rattled off the number. "Look, man, there's a good chance that if she's there she doesn't want to see you. I mean, if I'm reading the situation right."

"You are." Damn it, taking her to the club was a mistake. Gabe should have known business would intrude on their night, but he'd wanted to show her how his half lived. How it wasn't as terrifying and foreign as she believed. There's no way he could have anticipated Lynn showing up—or Elle jumping to the worst possible conclusion.

Look where that got him. "Thanks, Nathan."

"No problem. Fill me in tomorrow."

"Will do." Gabe hung up and barely waited for his screen to clear before he typed in the number. A female voice answered. "This is Roxanne."

He placed her as the same woman Elle had been out to dinner with the night he'd given her the flowers. She'd been on his side before, maybe she would this time too. "Roxanne, this is Gabe. I'm loo—" The phone clicked and went dead.

What the? Gabe shook it, frowning. No way she just hung up on him. Who did that? Gritting his teeth, he dialed again. This time it barely rang once. "What the hell do you want?"

Obviously she'd talked to Elle. That was good. It meant Elle was on the phone before she turned hers off. Which meant it was far less likely that she'd been hurt or attacked.

"Do you know where Elle is?"

"She doesn't want to talk to you."

Relief nearly sent Gabe off the road. She was okay. Pissed as hell, but okay. "Is she with you? Is she okay?"

"What are you talking about? Lord, I swear, men these days are idiots. Look, she doesn't want anything to do with you so just leave her the hell alone. Okay? Okay." *Click*.

Gabe forced his foot off the pedal and considered trying to track down where this Roxanne chick lived. No, he couldn't do that. Elle was probably freaked enough without him showing up to shake some sense into her like some crazed stalker.

Even if that was exactly how he felt right now.

Flipping a U-turn, he headed back north.
There was nothing else to do tonight but try to
outrace the demons in his head, every single one
of the bastards demanding he give up and let her
go. Elle thought she was too good for him. She
always had. She'd had her fill of slumming it, and
she was ready to get back to living the dream and
waiting for a gentleman to come along and sweep
her off her feet.

Well, fuck that. Didn't she realize true
gentlemen weren't the type to sweep anyone
anywhere? It was men like Gabe—the type of
man she labeled Neanderthal and wrote off—
who excelled at that sort of thing.

Well, he sure as hell wasn't done.

Gabe scrolled through his phone and dialed
Elle's number again. This time it rang. "Hello."
Christ, she'd been crying. He could hear it in her
voice.

"Elle."

"What do you want?"

Okay, so he hadn't been expecting her to
be okay with him after she'd taken off, but
the frostiness in her voice iced him out more
efficiently than if she'd hung up on him.

"Babe—"

"No, you don't get to call me that. Not

anymore."

Every word out of her mouth was a knife in his gut. "What the—"

But apparently she wasn't going to let him finish. "I don't want your explanation." She hesitated. "I don't want *you*."

So she was just going to sit on her throne of judgment and look down on him? The idiot woman was so sure she was right, she didn't want to hear anything he had to say. So be it. He'd never had to explain himself to country corn princesses before and he sure as hell wasn't going to start now. He didn't need this shit in his life.

Gabe should have kept his goddamn mouth shut, but it was too much on top of everything else. "Yeah? Because you didn't say that earlier tonight."

Elle made a sound that was half laugh, half sob. "You know what? Tonight you reaffirmed that I was right all along. So thank you for that. Next time I won't make the same mistake. Goodbye, Gabe." Her voice was so thick with tears, he could barely understand her. "Please don't call me again."

He kept the phone to his ear for a long time after she hung up. Gabe blinked, only now realizing that he'd been sitting at this stop sign ever since she picked up. He didn't know what to do. His first instinct was to track her down, but she sounded like she'd already made her decision. It didn't matter what he felt or how they'd connected or that things had been so great up until this shitstorm—Elle didn't want anything to do with him. She couldn't have made it clearer than if she spelled it out with her pink lipstick—the same fucking lipstick he couldn't stop thinking about.

Gabe shook his head, trying to clear the buzzing in his brain. He needed to get out of here, at least for a few days. Clear his mind. Figure out what he wanted. Do anything other than sit at this stop sign and let the pit inside his stomach swallow him whole.

Mind set, he drove to his place. The empty house seemed to taunt him as he walked the halls to his room. Here, faced with the physical manifestation of his loneliness, he knew he'd made the right decision to leave. Gabe went into his room and tossed a few changes of clothes in a carry-on bag. He'd go take care of the L.A. club, since *that* was one problem that he could solve.

It would give them both a few days to cool off, and then Gabe would figure out where to go from there. Maybe if he could sit her down long enough, he could explain the entire situation. She'd have to see reason once she realized what she'd walked in on. Then again, Elle hadn't exactly shown herself as willing to listen to reason. Maybe it was better that he cut his losses now.

It would be so easy to take off, tour his clubs, and do whatever it took to get that damn woman out of his system. If he kept busy, he could probably even ignore the barbs slicing their way through his chest.

• • •

Stupid. She was so damn stupid. Elle pulled the blanket more tightly around herself. God help her, but if Roxanne said "I told you so" she was going to lose her mind. "And then I took off."

The brunette passed over a steaming cup of green tea, her green eyes sympathetic. "I'm sorry, honey."

Words bubbled up, poison she couldn't keep inside her any longer. "I feel like a *whore*."

"Oh jeez. You are not. You're a woman."

"A woman like freaking Jezebel."

Roxanne settled into the love seat and shook her head. "I hardly think Jezebel was this dramatic."

Hurt lanced through her, the pain barely scratching the surface of her agony over Gabe. She'd changed when she was with him, had become someone…a person who stopped overthinking things—and now look what happened. "Whose side are you on?"

"Yours, sweetie. Always yours. But this is your crazy-ass mother talking. You know I hate it when I hear her words coming out of your mouth. You aren't a whore, you're human. Hard to believe you aren't perfect, but such is life."

More tears—she had an endless supply, it seemed—bubbled up. Elle tried and failed to hold back a sob. "I w-was happy w-with him." That was the worst part—she'd *liked* the person she became when she was around Gabe. And he was lying to her the entire time. Unforgivable.

"I know." Roxanne sipped her tea. "What are you going to do?"

The question of her life. Things used to be so simple—she wanted her career, her husband, a couple of kids, a good life. Now…now, Elle didn't know what she wanted. "I'm not sure."

"He's going to keep calling. You realize that, right?"

"I'm not ready to talk to him." She wasn't

sure she'd ever be ready. Every time she thought of Gabe, she saw the red lipstick on his cheek. Maybe not talking to him was better. It was certainly safer.

"Okay. I'll field the phone calls for the time being."

"Thank you." She tried and failed to dredge up a smile. "Can I…Can I stay here until Monday?"

"Of course."

Roxanne couldn't be her protector forever. Eventually Elle had to go back into the real world and deal with this. She had no illusions about Gabe's tenacity—he'd found her before, and he would again. The trick was to figure out what the hell she'd say to his face when he did. "Maybe I can just take a vacation or something. I'm sure Florida is really nice this time of year."

"Honey, it's hurricane season."

There went that plan. Elle slouched deeper into the couch. "I could go visit Ian in Japan."

"He's only there for another few weeks."

"Don't remind me." As much as she wanted to see her big brother, she really didn't want to have to explain everything that happened with Gabe. He'd go ballistic if he found out about *any* of this. Yeah, better if he lived on in blissful ignorance. Which meant she'd need a good story to tell him before this was all over. Elle sighed. "Canada?"

"Three things." Roxanne held up three fingers. "Bears, mountain lions, and badgers."

A pathetic laugh escaped. "I don't think badgers should be on the top three things to avoid in Canada."

"Think what you want." She shuddered. "Those things are terrifying."

The absurdity of Roxanne being afraid of badgers of all things shook off some of her bad mood. Elle actually succeeded in smiling this time around. "I'm sure there's a way around that. Just stick to the cities."

"Let's just take Canada off the list and call it good, okay?"

"Fine." She sighed. "Guess I have to stay in town and figure this out, don't I?"

"Hate to be the one to tell you this, but I'm pretty sure that Neanderthal of yours would chase you across the wilds of Canada." Roxanne shuddered. "Then you'd be dealing with him *and* badgers. Let's just not."

"Good plan. Let's definitely not. And he's not *my* anything. He more than proved that tonight." She could deal with this. Really, she could.

In the meantime, she was going to let

Roxanne distract her with talking about anything but sex in storage closets and Gabe.

• • •

"I'm sick. Really sick." Elle forced a cough.

"You are not." Nathan didn't sound the least bit sympathetic. "You're avoiding coming into work."

Well, crap. She swallowed hard. "I just…I can't."

"Elle, you don't have to worry about running into him. He's not even here. He's in L.A."

Of course he was. Gabe hadn't even waited two days before he went running back to his other woman. Elle hadn't thought she could hurt any more, but the shards in her heart twisted viciously. "Oh."

Nathan sighed. "Come in. I'll have coffee waiting for you." He hung up before she could come up with another excuse.

Elle couldn't bring herself to put forth her usual effort into getting ready for work. She pulled on a sundress and threw her hair into a ponytail and called it good. Really, who was there for her to impress? She didn't care if Nathan saw her as less than perfect. Heck, he already knew the truth. She was a fool, willing to believe any lie as long as it sounded halfway convincing.

No. No more beating herself up. She made a mistake, she should have known better, but it was over now.

Nathan looked up as she walked into the gallery. "Forgive me if I sound like an ass, but you look like shit."

"You're not helping." She paused in front of her favorite painting, but even it couldn't ease the ache in her chest. Taking the coffee cup he offered, she sank into the chair behind her desk. She'd barely sat down when her phone rang. Elle nearly groaned out loud when she looked at the caller ID. Ian. Taking a deep breath, she forced herself to smile. "Hey, big brother."

"You never called me back."

Yeah, because she didn't know what to say. "I was embarrassed about how our last conversation went."

"Ellie, I was worried about you."

"I'm sorry. Everything's fine now. It was a momentary weakness." And not one she planned on repeating, no matter how good Gabe made her feel when they were together.

"It didn't sound like a momentary weakness. It sounded like some asshole broke your heart."

"You know me, I pick winners." She started to laugh, but stopped when the sound cracked unnaturally.

"Jason wasn't your fault."

"What's that saying? The definition of insanity is doing the same thing over and over, and expecting different results."

Ian took a deep breath. "You're not insane and you're not stupid. Jason was a piece of shit."

Elle shook her head. "It doesn't matter anymore. Honestly, though, I'm a lot better. We broke up, and I haven't seen him since."

"I didn't even realize you were dating someone."

She didn't know if what she and Gabe had would count as dating, but she wasn't going to tell Ian that they'd just been having sex. "Yeah, we haven't talked much lately." And he'd never understand.

"I'm sorry, Ellie. Really sorry." There were voices in the background. Ian sighed. "I have to go. Drills, you know? I'll call you soon. Love you."

"Love you, too." She hung up, not sure if she felt better or worse for having talked to him. She took a drink of coffee and sat back with a sigh. Time to get to work.

. . .

"What are you going to do?"

Gabe barely resisted the urge to throw his phone across the room. He swore to God, if his brother asked him that one more time he was going to do something they'd both regret. "I don't know." He'd spent the weekend putting out fires in L.A. The old G.M. hadn't acted so tough once they sat down in a room together. It'd taken all of twenty minutes to get him to sign an agreement saying it had been a lawful termination, probably because he didn't try to intimidate Gabe the way he had with Lynn. After that, there'd been half a dozen smaller problems waiting for him to deal with.

"I don't know what I'm going to do. I guess I'm going to try to talk to her." And hope it went better than last time. He kept picturing the horror on her face, which quickly melted into the exact same expression she'd worn the moment she turned on the light and realized he wasn't Nathan. "Maybe this was a mistake."

Something rustled on the line. "You're being stupid."

"I am not. She and I are too different."

"Not true. Did you ever think that the reason you work so well together is because you're so different?"

Of course he had. It was part of the reason he'd pursued her. He'd thought she was everything he ever wanted. Gabe wasn't sure he'd been mistaken. "It's not that simple."

"Are you trying to convince me or yourself? Because you're doing a piss-poor job of both. Just figure your shit out and win her back. Simple."

"So simple that you let your mystery chick slip through your damn fingertips?"

Gabe had always thought the expression "you could hear a pin drop" was exaggerating. He was wrong. So wrong. The silence was almost physical between them, a wall he had no hope of climbing.

Nathan finally said, "I'm going to pretend you didn't say that, and we're going to move on. Figure your shit out, Gabe, because I'm tired of your anger coming out at me."

The worst part of it was he was right. Gabe should have let it go. "I'm sorry."

For a long second he actually thought Nathan would say it wasn't okay. "I'm not worried about it."

"You see how it is? This chick has me so

twisted up, I can't see straight anymore. It's not natural."

"Do you care about her?"

He didn't even have to think about his answer. "Yeah. A lot."

"Well, she cares about you, too. She tried to call in sick today and, when she finally showed up, she looked like shit warmed over."

"I'm sure she's fine."

"Will you get over yourself? So she thought the worst of you, so what? You guys had only known each other two weeks—two really rocky weeks. And even after the multiple screwups, she gave you another chance. Don't you think you need to get off your high horse and do the same for her?"

When he put it like that, he made Gabe feel like an idiot. "You're a pain in my ass."

"No. That's the stick you have shoved up there. You need to stop pussyfooting around and figure out your big move."

The worst part was that his brother might actually be right. Sure, Elle had run screaming into the night at the first indication that he might be less than Prince Charming, but hadn't he done the same damn thing? A sobering thought if there ever was one. Which meant one of them had to be the bigger person, and put aside their pride. Gabe rubbed his jaw. Ah hell. If he didn't try, he'd always wonder what could have happened.

Anything he did would have to be pretty damn big to get Elle back on his side—and in his bed. Gabe turned a slow circle, mind whirling. The normal "I'm an asshole and I'm sorry" gifts wouldn't do anything. Chocolates, flowers, jewelry, none of it would make Elle stop long enough to listen to him. But there was one thing that would, something she wanted more than anything. He leaned against the desk. "I have an idea. It's a Hail Mary, but it's all I've got."

In just two weeks, his entire world had been rocked. Elle had shown up, bringing a breath of fresh air he hadn't even known he needed. Gabe didn't want to go back to the emptiness his life had been before her—the free space between work was a time he avoided like the plague. With her, he actually looked forward to something other than his clubs and tattoo shop.

It was time to win back his woman.

CHAPTER TWENTY-TWO

Elle stopped in her driveway to stare at the package leaning against her front door. Judging from the basic brown paper, twine wrapping, and its size, it was some kind of painting.

What was it doing *here*?

Except she couldn't pretend she didn't know. There was only one person who'd be leaving her things on the front doorstep, and she didn't want anything to do with him right now. A week sure as heck wasn't long enough to sort out how she felt. A *year* wouldn't be long enough.

With a sigh, she unlocked the door and carted the package inside. A cowardly voice insisted she toss it in the garbage, but that was freaking rude, no matter who gave the present. Elle settled for tucking it behind the sofa. She'd deal with it later—when she wasn't on the verge of bursting into tears. Lord, she was a mess.

As the night wore on, Elle couldn't settle down. She moved from one part of the house to the other—trying to zone out with a book until it became obvious she couldn't focus on the words, poking through the fridge but deciding she wasn't hungry after all—before finally trudging upstairs to fold laundry. Faced with a huge pile of clean clothes, she decided she didn't really want to do that either. Nothing could hold her interest.

She needed to do something about it.

No, she didn't want to see. It had to be from Gabe—he didn't deserve the time and effort it would take her to go downstairs and unwrap it.

Back and forth she went. Should she throw it out or sit up here and pretend it didn't exist? Yeah, 'cause the last one was working out so well. Finally, completely disgusted with herself, Elle picked up her phone. It rang a few times before Roxanne answered. "Rox, I need you."

"What happened?"

"I think Gabe left something here for me. I'm…afraid to open it."

Roxanne sighed and Elle loved her all the more for not hanging up right then and there. "I'm on my way."

"I love you, Rox."

"Yeah, you too." She hung up, probably cursing Elle up one side and down the other in her head.

Elle sat on her bed, rocking back and forth, until she heard the front door open. For one insane moment, she was sure Gabe had come back and every cell in her body leapt to life. But then Roxanne's voice echoed through the house, "Elle?"

"Up here."

"Uh-huh. Right. I'm assuming this is the painting? I'll just get to it."

The sound of ripping paper had Elle up and off the bed in record time. She ran down the stairs to find Roxanne setting the painting on the kitchen island. For several breaths, she refused to reconcile what she was seeing. "That's…"

"Yes, it looks like the same painting you've been obsessed with for months." Roxanne tilted her head to the side. "I mean, it's pretty enough, but I don't really see the appeal."

"It's…" She couldn't even begin to find the words to express her emotions. Good lord, she didn't even know what she was feeling right now. Elle had seen the price tag on this piece—she'd agonized over the reality that she'd never be able to afford it. Not in a million years.

Gabe bought it for her.

"I have to take it back."

Roxanne gave her a look like she'd lost her mind. "What are you talking about?"

"I can't take this. It's too much."

"Honey, listen to yourself." Elle made a grab for the painting, but she easily held it out of reach. "Stop for a second and think about this. How long have you wanted this painting?"

"Five months."

Roxanne dodged another wild reach. "And could you have ever bought it for yourself?"

"No! That's the point." Elle smacked her hip on the corner of the island hard enough to bruise. Ouch. "He can't freaking *buy me off.*"

"I really don't think that's what he's trying to do." When Elle's mouth dropped open, she handed over a sealed envelope. "Look, I get that you have crazy-conflicted feelings about this guy, but I'd have to be blind not to see that he's crazy about you. The least you can do is read what he wrote."

Elle backed away as if the envelope were going to reach out and bite her. Heck, maybe it was. "I don't want to hear what he has to say."

"Then you're an idiot."

That stopped her in her tracks. "Whose side arc you on?"

"Are you even listening to yourself? You're pissed off at him for…what exactly? For wiping lipstick off his face? It's not like you found him banging that bitch against the wall. For being too much like Jason? Because I don't really see how he's all that similar to your pissant of an ex-boyfriend. For leaving you? Honey, you're the one who took off and told him to lose your number. Or maybe it was for giving you multiple mind-blowing orgasms? Because that doesn't sound all that bad either, Elle." Roxanne set the painting down and smoothed her hair back. "I love you, but this is ridiculous. Did the man make you happy?"

She wanted to say no, but she couldn't lie to her best friend. "Yes."

"Then, again, what's the problem?"

"He lied to me."

"Did he? Or did you take off before he had a chance to explain?"

"I saw him kissing that woman."

"You saw him wiping off her lipstick. Look, it's simple. Are you really going to throw away a chance to be happy based on what might be a misunderstanding?"

"It's not a misunderstanding." It wasn't.

Was it?

"Whatever you have to tell yourself, sweetie. I'm going home." Roxanne turned and walked out of the room, leaving Elle staring after her.

Great, now she'd managed to alienate the last person on earth sympathetic to her cause. She used the corner of the painting to rotate it toward her. As usual, its beauty actually took Elle's breath away. If Gabe was really trying to buy her off, he was doing a darn good job of it. Only one way to tell for sure, though. She inched the envelope closer, taking in the total lack of decoration. It didn't even have her name on it. Then again, who else would it be for?

And, yeah, she was totally stalling.

Holding her breath, she tore into it and pulled out the letter. Elle choked on a laugh. Of course it was written on lined paper and ripped out of a spiral notebook. Why did she even bother being surprised? A part of her wanted to be derisive — seriously, couldn't he put a little bit of effort into some stationery? — but the rest of her smothered the voice. Gabe had just given her the single most overwhelming gift of her life, worlds better than any guy she'd ever dated. Biting her lip, she started to read.

Then the meaning of his words hit. She groped for the kitchen stool, unable to tear her eyes from the page. This wasn't a gloating "Look what I bought you! I done good" letter. No, this was something else entirely. Elle read it twice, set it down, and then picked it up again. Surely he wasn't serious. She looked at the painting and then back to the letter. Oh yeah, he was serious.

Elle,

Babe, I wish I knew what to say to make this better, but we both know I'm no good with words. So I'll tell you what I'm feeling right now, and then you can decide where you stand. I know this whole thing with me hasn't been what you've imagined dating should be, and I'm really goddamn sorry for the other night. I know you won't believe me, but I swear to God nothing happened with Lynn. She's the manager of my L.A. club and was up here because I'd been blowing off my responsibilities to be with you. She kissed me on the cheek like she always does. Nothing more, nothing less.

All that shit aside, I care about you. Hell, woman, I'm falling for you, hard and fast, and I don't even know which way is up anymore. I mean, Christ, I felt like I'd won the lotto when you crawled into my bed, but being with you has turned into so much more than mind-blowing sex. You make me want things I've never allowed myself to want before, and you've made me happier than I've been in years.

I'm sorry, babe, really sorry. Please forgive me. I just found you. I don't want to lose you.

—Gabe

It wasn't a declaration of love, but she wouldn't have believed him if he'd tried that angle. No, this wasn't an angle at all. Just pure Gabe. Elle pressed the paper to her lips, her mind whirling. He was falling for her. She made him happy, made him want to settle down. She wasn't alone in this sideways emotional spiral.

Setting the letter back on the counter, she focused on the painting. A token of how crazy he was about her—not him trying to buy her off. God, Roxanne had been right. She was so busy living in the past, she'd jumped to the worst possible conclusion without giving him a chance to explain. And if she'd trusted him the way he deserved, he wouldn't have even needed to explain anything. Realizing that made her feel like a heel. All this time she'd been so sure he was in complete control, was toying with her, but it had just been her personal fears at work.

It was a lot to think about. Elle walked upstairs and into the spare bedroom. The painting she'd started that morning two weeks ago still stood, half-covered, exactly where she'd left it. She crossed the room in halting steps and pulled the sheet off. Even after having only seen him the one time, she'd captured the muscle tone of his chest and breadth of his shoulders. Gabe had certainly made an impression.

She skimmed over the memories of their time together, focusing on the morning after the allergic reaction. He'd bared his soul to her about his past, about his mother. *That* had been the truth.

Her taste in men wasn't as bad as she thought.

Which meant she needed to figure out how to make this right. Elle picked up her brush and moved to the canvas. It was time to finish what she'd begun. She just needed to find the courage to take that step.

CHAPTER TWENTY-THREE

The low buzz of tattoo guns usually soothed Gabe, but today he wanted to throw them through the window. Two days. Two goddamn days he'd been back in town and hc hadn't heard a single thing. He propped his feet on the chair and wondered what he was even doing here. It seemed like a decent idea at the time—he didn't want to be alone, so he came into the shop. But all it'd done was remind him how unnecessary he was here. Somehow, over the years, he'd become more guest artist than a regular, all his time spent on the nightclubs. It had never bothered him before, but now it was like he didn't have a single goddamn thing holding him in town.

Maybe he should take off, catch the next flight to Seattle. He could hop down the coast and visit the clubs he hadn't been to in a while. Anything to keep his mind off how much he ached. Who would have thought that two fucking weeks would be enough to send him spiraling over some chick?

The bell above the door jingled, and he nearly fell out of his chair when he saw her walk into his shop. He must have been dreaming, damn it. There was no way this was happening.

Why was she here? He tried to ask, but couldn't get his mouth to work as Elle crossed the shiny wooden floor to stand before him. The woman was a vision, her long dress hugging every curve and leaving her shoulders bare. The bright tropical print set off her sun-kissed skin and blond hair, and all he wanted in that moment was to yank her into his lap and hold her until he was sure this was real. No. That wasn't right. He shouldn't be thinking about touching her—not when things had ended so shitty last time.

"Hi."

Right, he should be talking right now. Gabe jumped up. "What are you doing here?" What a thing to say. Shit. "Damn it, that's not what I meant." He really didn't want to do this where both his artists and their clients could see, but there was nowhere else to go unless he wanted to have this conversation in the bathroom. Christ, what was he even thinking? The woman made him crazy.

Why was she here?

Elle actually smiled. "I got your package." One of the guys laughed, and her face went crimson. "Er, you know what I mean. It was too much."

So she'd come here to argue about it. Gabe sank into his rolling chair, his stomach tied up in knots. This woman made him feel like he was back in high school, a bumbling fool who couldn't do anything right.

"But…the note was unexpected." She glanced at the other people in the shop, all now blatantly watching them. For a second, he thought she'd bail, but she squared her shoulders and spoke in a rush. "I finished my painting."

Gabe blinked. "Painting."

"Yes, a painting." Her hands did a nervous flutter. "It's one I started the day after we, well, you know." Elle looked up and met his gaze. "Of you. I'd, ah, like you to come over and give me your opinion."

A painting? Of him? Could that mean… Gabe shoved to his feet. "Let's go."

"Hold on." She pushed him back into his

chair. "I'm really, really sorry that I freaked out on you. Remember that guy who my brother beat up? Well, I fell head-over-heels for him and he was a bad boy like you. Only not like you, because you're really not like him at all. He didn't care about me, and all he wanted was to get into my pants, and apparently the pants of every other girl on campus while he was dating me. But then he broke up with me and made sure to do it in front of my friends in the most humiliating way possible." Christ, he'd known that dude was an asshole, but Gabe hadn't expected this. She took a deep breath, and rushed on before he could reach for her. "Basically, what I'm trying to say is that my trust issues aren't your fault, but I took them out on you anyway. Please forgive me."

"Ancient history, babe. I want to see this painting." A painting *of him*.

"There's more."

More? What could there possibly be more of? But she rushed on before he could get the courage to give his question voice.

"I'm here for a tattoo."

The woman was moving too fast for him to keep up. "A tattoo."

"Yes, a tattoo."

None of this made any sense. "What would

your mother think?"

"I don't care what my mother thinks." Elle put her hands on her hips. "You know, you're not making this easy."

It was like they were having a conversation and he was only hearing part of it. "I don't get it. Why do you want a tattoo? Why *here*?"

"Were you serious about the stuff you wrote?"

Hell, he'd spent hours agonizing over that stupid letter and the damn thing didn't even take up half a page. "Yeah, I was."

She let out a breath. "Well, it turns out I'm falling for you, too. And you make me really, really happy."

Gabe's mouth fell open.

"You see," she continued before he could say anything, "after the really traumatic stuff with my ex, I thought my taste in men couldn't be trusted. My mother enthusiastically agreed, which is why she's been trying to push me into relationships with 'respectable' men for the last few years. But the funny thing is, if I'd have been brave enough to trust my instincts, you're exactly who I would have picked for myself."

"I—what?" She would have picked *him*. Gabe blinked at her, distantly wondering how often she was going to sucker punch him like this…or if he even minded.

"Yes, Gabe. I would have picked you. I *do* pick you." She gave him a nervous smile. "And it's the best decision I've ever made."

He was pretty sure the floor just fell out from underneath him. This was definitely a dream. No way in reality would Elle come walking into his shop and tell him she was falling for him. That she'd pick him over everyone else. That kind of shit didn't happen to guys like him.

When he didn't say anything, she took a deep breath. "So…remember that conversation we had at dinner? The one where we talked about people getting tattoos to remember certain things?"

"Yes." As if he'd forget any of their time together—not when he'd spent all his time poring over every single moment of it.

"Well, that's why I want a tattoo. Because I feel like my entire life has been turned on its head since I met you. I thought I was playing it safe, but really I was hiding. I'm not going to hide anymore. If that's not something to commemorate, I don't know what is."

Gabe held out his hand, still half-sure she wasn't serious. But then Elle slipped her hand into his and it hit him—this was *real*. She was here and actually saying these things. He pulled her into his lap, and she didn't even shriek in protest. Instead, she settled there as if this were the most natural thing in the world. "You're serious?"

Elle cupped his face with one hand. "I'm serious. I'm falling for you, Gabe Schultz, and I would very much like you to tattoo me."

It was only then he noticed the paper in her other hand. Settling her more firmly in his lap, he took the paper. It was an exact replica of the painting he'd bought her. "This is some serious work."

"I thought we could start small." She pointed to the flower on the shoulder blade of the woman in the picture. "Maybe see how things go and work from there."

Yeah, they weren't just talking about tattoos. "Just so happens, my schedule is cleared for the day." Even if it hadn't been, he would have canceled on the president for this woman. He pulled her closer, loving the feel of her hips under his hands. It was like the perfect Christmas morning he'd never had as a child. The one where he woke up to realize he'd gotten the one thing he always wanted.

Elle kissed him, right there in front of

everyone. Her tongue traced his, unbearably sweet despite the way she set him on fire. And she wanted him. Gabe wanted to shout it to the world. He gentled the kiss, finally leaning back with a grin. "You ready, babe? This is a big step."

She kissed him again. "I'll be in your hands, so I think I'm good. Let's do this."

EPILOGUE

"Maybe we should wait." Elle tried not to fidget as Gabe drove. They'd left the highway fifteen minutes ago, winding deeper into the country. Closer to her parents' house. She caught herself twisting her dress and forced her hands still. "It's only been a few months. We could cancel and wait for…Thanksgiving. Thanksgiving would be a great time to meet my parents." Her mother would be running the kitchen, far too busy to interrogate Elle's new boyfriend.

Boyfriend. Even two months later, it still felt like she was dreaming. She reached over and laced her fingers through his, just because she could.

Gabe squeezed her hand. "Babe, I'm not scared of your parents."

"That's only because you haven't met them yet." Oh, her dad was laid back and would probably really like Gabe. Her mom...not so much.

"I have to meet them sometime. Might as well be tonight."

She took a deep breath, searching for some of the calm he seemed to have no trouble finding. He was right. Her mother had become more and more determined to meet this mystery man of Elle's, and she wasn't going to be put off again. Which wouldn't be so bad if Elle could be sure how she'd react.

Before she had a chance to figure out what she was going to do, Gabe pulled into her parents' driveway. The wheels crunched over gravel, and she couldn't help a little smile at the memories of a childhood spent running free out here. She could swear there were whole summers that she'd spent barefoot with Ian. It was one of the few times her dad successfully vetoed her mom—he'd claimed it was an important part of growing up. Those were some of the best summers of her life.

Gabe parked and turned to face her. "It'll be fine. We'll have a great dinner, and then I'll take you home and we'll christen... What room haven't we hit yet?"

It said something that Elle had to actually think about it. She blushed. "Um, maybe the laundry room?"

A slow grin spread over his face, making her heart speed up. "Then we'll go home and play with the spin cycle."

The image immediately sprang into her mind—Elle sitting on the washing machine, her legs wrapped around his waist, and him thrusting into her as the machine vibrated. "Oh lordy."

"Just think about that whenever it seems like dinner will never end."

"You're evil." She kissed him, her tongue tracing his. Would she ever get tired of this? She doubted it—the taste of Gabe always sent her entire body into overdrive. Reluctantly, she pulled back. It would be just her luck to have one of her parents come knocking on the steamed-up window. She licked her lips and tried not to sound breathy. "I think I like it."

"You *do* like it." Gabe got out of the car and walked around to open her door. She was pretty sure she'd never get tired of him doing that, either. As they walked up the stairs to the wraparound porch, he took her hand again, almost as if he knew how much she needed the grounding.

It wasn't that she was afraid of her parents—or ashamed of Gabe. She wasn't. It was more that she didn't know what her mother would do or say. Filter was not a word in the woman's vocabulary. Gabe said he didn't care what her mom thought of him, but what if her mom went off the deep end like she'd done before? Elle had seen grown men hunch their shoulders as if they were trying to make themselves smaller targets in the face of her pointed comments. The thought of Gabe being the focus of that ire wasn't a comfortable one.

Elle gave herself a mental shake. No. She'd made her decision. Gabe was the one she wanted. While she wanted her mother's approval, it wasn't as vital as she'd once thought. And if her mother thought she could scare off the man of Elle's dreams, she had another think coming. She wasn't going to give Gabe up. Not for anyone.

Thankfully, it was her dad who opened the door. He engulfed her in a cookie-scented bear hug. He always seemed to smell like holiday sweets, as if he'd escaped from the North Pole or something. "It's been too long, Ellie." After he set her back on her feet, he gave Gabe a long look. "And you're the boyfriend we keep hearing so much about."

"Sir." He shook her father's hand. "I'm Gabe Schultz."

"Nice to meet you." Some judgment passed through her dad's eyes, but Elle couldn't be sure which way it had gone. *Didn't matter*, she told herself. Gabe was *hers*, darn it. But then, when he ushered them in, her dad paused long enough to wink at her. Relief made her stomach flutter. He liked Gabe. Though *how* he knew he liked Gabe after five seconds was a mystery. They'd barely exchanged five words. Shouldn't he wait until they actually sat down and talked before he gave his approval?

She was overthinking things. She needed to cut that out.

Her dad led them into the formal dining room. Crap. She'd hoped dinner would be set up in the nook, where the family usually ate. Apparently her mom was pulling out all the stops for this one, though. Before Elle could decide if that was a good thing or a bad thing, the woman herself swept into the room, wearing her June Cleaver outfit. Though June Cleaver had never worn an expression quite so unforgiving.

"Daughter."

Oh good God, this was going to get ugly.

Swallowing past her suddenly dry throat, she said, "Mom. This is Gabe, my boyfriend."

"Yes, I do remember you using that word. Odd how you acquire a boyfriend and I don't see you for two months."

There went the guilt trip. Elle shot a look at Gabe, but his face gave away nothing. "Ma'am, it's a pleasure to meet you."

"I truly doubt that." Her fingers barely touched Gabe's hand before she turned away, effectively dismissing him as unimportant without saying a single word.

Elle stared. Even during her worst days, her mother had never been so outright rude. "Mother, you—"

"Let's get dinner on the table." Her mother swept out of the room, somehow managing to make it an insult.

Her dad shrugged. "Sorry, Ellie. She's been in rare form for days."

"She's being rude." As soon as the words were out, it was everything she could do not to slap a hand over her mouth. She'd never verbally criticized her mom. *Never*.

"Why don't we sit?" Gabe's fingers brushed her arm, centering her. They'd get through this. It didn't matter if her mom approved—Elle had made her choice—but her mother didn't have to go out of her way to make everyone uncomfortable.

"So, Gabe, what does running a line of nightclubs entail?" her dad asked as he got settled into his chair. "It sounds like exciting business."

Gabe smiled. If she hadn't spent a really embarrassing amount of time staring at his face, she wouldn't have noticed the tightness around his eyes. "I'd guess it's a lot like running any other business. Managing expenses, marketing, and trying to keep everything out of the red. I spend the majority of my time in an office, so not all that exciting."

Considering they'd just taken a trip down to Portland to iron out an issue with the assistant general manager that had ended with a screaming match between him and one of the bartenders, Gabe wasn't being one hundred percent honest. Then again, she didn't really want to get into it with her parents either. Elle caught his eye, and raised her brows. "Yes, Gabe. Your work is absolutely tedious."

"Very." The corners of his mouth canted up. "What about you, Mr. Walser? Elle is remarkably closemouthed when it comes to the family's business."

"That's most likely because it bores her to death." Her dad laughed, the sound containing none of the censure her mom's would have. "We own 600-odd acres out here and specialize in organic produce. There's quite the market for it these days."

This was good. Her dad could go on about the pros of organic food for hours if left unchecked. All she and Gabe would have to do is sit here and nod at the right intervals. Dinner would be cake. Elle's stomach had barely unknotted when her mom marched back into the room, carrying a platter with a roast and cooked vegetables. She literally turned up her nose at Gabe. Elle's jaw dropped. Even with Jason, her mom hadn't been so...snooty. This had to stop. Now.

"Mom—"

Gabe laid a hand on her knee and shot her a look, instantly quelling Elle's words. Apparently she was supposed to sit here and let her mom keep insulting him. Under different circumstances, Elle would have been more than happy to keep her head down. But this was *Gabe* her mom was trying to run off. She couldn't let that happen.

"Dinner looks wonderful, Mrs. Walser." He attempted a smile.

"Yes, well, you shouldn't get used to it. My daughter can't cook."

The tension in his hand was the only outward sign of Gabe's annoyance. To everyone else at the table, he looked pleasantly amused. "That won't be a problem, ma'am. I cook."

Her mom sank into the chair next to her dad. Glaciers were warmer than her smile. "I'm sure you do."

Her father frowned. "Now Elizabeth—"

"No, Charles. You'd don't get to 'now Elizabeth' me."

Her mom snapped out the words with far more venom than Elle had ever heard her use. What the heck was going on? Surely she wasn't this angry about *Gabe*?

Silence descended over the table. Desperate, Elle groped for a subject. "I've got news. Gabe finally convinced me to show Nathan some of my paintings, and he's going to put up two of them in the gallery."

She chose not to mention that one of the paintings was of Gabe. It was by far her best work, even better than the one she'd gifted him after her tattoo. She rolled her shoulders, thankful that the weather had cooled off enough to justify a sweater. As bad as things were now, they'd be so much worse if her mom caught sight of the tattoo covering her shoulder. "It's a fabulous opportunity. Countless artists have used Nathan's gallery to launch their careers."

"That's fantastic, honey." Her dad smiled and speared a huge piece of roast beef.

Her mom, of course, missed nothing. Her blue eyes flicked over first Gabe and then Elle. "These are like the landscapes you gave me for my birthday?"

"Ah…" Elle ignored Gabe's look. He knew how much she hated landscapes. It was on the tip of her tongue to lie to her mom, but she swallowed it down. If she couldn't be honest about how she chose to pursue her dream, then what was the point? Elle cleared her throat. "These are different. Male portraits."

"Male portraits." Her mom sniffed. "I suppose this new boyfriend is behind the change as well."

"Mom, he's sitting right here." Shock made Elle ignore Gabe squeezing her leg. "You're being rude."

"I'm merely making an observation."

"You're quite observant, Mrs. Walser." Despite

the tension in the room, Gabe sounded completely calm—amused, even. Someday she was going to have to learn that trick. He started making circles on her thigh, soothing her even though he was obviously angry. "Maybe with all your observations, you've noticed that your daughter is brilliant at painting portraits. They're her passion. Since you obviously care very much for your daughter, I'd think you'd want her to follow her dream."

Her mom's eyes flashed. "Cheeky, aren't you? I seem to remember another of my daughter's boyfriends who had a mouth on him. And look how that ended."

Elle started to speak, but Gabe beat her to the punch. "The worthless cheater? I've heard."

"Then you understand my reservations."

"Mom—"

"Your reservations are based on superficial similarities." Gabe sat back, taking the comfort of his touch with him. "It so happens that I love your daughter and I fully intend on spending the rest of my life with her."

All the breath left Elle's body in a rush, leaving her lightheaded and in danger of passing out. Maybe she should put her head between her legs? She blindly reached out, nearly knocking over her glass of water before her hand closed around it. She took a hurried sip as Gabe continued. "Which is why I fully intend on asking you for permission for her hand in marriage."

She spit out the water. "*What?*"

Gabe shrugged, apparently unconcerned that she'd just made a fool of herself with the water. "You're it for me, babe. I'd be an idiot to let you slip through my fingers."

"But…marriage." Her entire world narrowed down to Gabe. She could hear her mom sputtering, but none of the words penetrated. "That's a big step."

He laced his fingers through hers and raised them to kiss her knuckles. "I want forever with you."

Forever. She actually took half a second to picture what her life could be like if they were married. A home. The ability to spend as much time together as they wanted without having to pick which house to go to. Kids. Gabe's kids. *Forever.* Oh lordy, she wanted it all so badly. Elle smiled, tears pricking her eyes. "I want forever with you, too."

"*Over my dead body.*"

Elle jerked her hand out of Gabe's grasp. "Mother!"

Her mom pushed back her chair and stood.

"I'd like to speak to you in the kitchen, daughter.
Alone."

It might have been phrased as a request but
only an idiot would see it as something other
than an order. Her mom wanted to talk? Fine.
Elle had some things she needed to say. She
stood, hurrying for the kitchen before she could
lose her nerve. As it was, she nearly threw caution
to the wind and sprinted for the front door—
probably would have if Gabe didn't have his keys.

The kitchen was the site of so many
childhood lectures on how a proper lady
behaves—sex in a storage closet wasn't on that
list—and failed cooking lessons. As usual, her
mother stood on the other side of the island, her
arms crossed over her chest. She looked like the
perfect housewife, her faded blond hair pulled
into an effortless updo, her makeup without
smudges, and her skirt and sweater completely
above reproach. Not that anyone would ever
have the guts to reproach Elizabeth Walser, but
she made darn sure no one had a leg to stand on.
And, right now, those pale pink lips were pressed
together in anger.

With a sigh, Elle sank onto her customary
stool. She wasn't going to be able to get a word
in edgewise until her mom had her say. "Yes,

Mother?"

"Elle Laurie, what is the meaning of this?"

Even though she'd prepared for it, Elle still winced at the question. "Mom, I love him."

"I thought we'd reached an understanding. Look what happened last time you picked a man for yourself. You spent months depressed and struggling to get out of bed after that ended. *Months*. And you only dated him—you weren't fool enough to marry him. I refuse to go through it again."

It was an effort to keep her voice steady. While her mother had a point about Jason, Gabe was another person entirely. "He's different."

"Yes, yes. I'm sure he's a gentleman who would never break your heart, or run around on you, or beat you down as a person. Not at all." Her mom threw up her hands. "I swear, sometimes you don't have the sense God gave a child."

"*Enough*."

Her mom started to speak, then frowned. "Excuse me, what did you just say?"

"I said… No."

She blinked. "No?"

It was now or never. If she didn't get this out, she'd never be able to live with herself. "Mom, I love you, but you have to stop. You haven't even given him a chance and already you're acting like you have his number." Which was exactly what Elle had done when they first met. The similarity stuck in her throat. Oh God, she'd been turning into her mother. "He's never been anything but respectful to me, and *he's* never cornered me and tried to stick his hand up my skirt after repeatedly being turned down. Which is exactly what Sam Masterson Jr. did on our first date."

"Elle—"

"Let me finish." When her mom's mouth shut, Elle charged on. "He's kind and sweet, and he's built a business from nothing. He loves me, despite the fact that I treated him like you just did when we met." Best not to get into the exact circumstances of their meeting. "He wants forever with me, Mom. And, you know what? I'm really freaking proud of my paintings and you should be, too. If you can't support me in this—in *all* of it—then we have nothing more to talk about."

Her mom's eyes went wide. "What's this man done to you that you'd abandon your family?"

"It's not what he's done to me. It's not what anyone's done to me. But I'm not going to have my life ruled by you or anyone else."

"I just want you to be happy," her mom whispered.

"I am happy—really, truly happy. Why can't *you* just be happy for me?" Pressure built in Elle's chest, until she wanted to scream with it. Instead, her voice came out remarkably subdued. "Do Gabe and I need to leave?"

Her mom seemed to gather herself. She smoothed her clothes and patted at the nonexistent hairs out of place on her head. "No, that won't be necessary."

Elle's mother, backing down? She couldn't quite believe it. "You're going to be supportive?"

"You've obviously made your decision. If he truly makes you happy, then I'll have to abide by it, no matter what I think." Her mom sighed. It wasn't exactly the most heartening statement, but it was better than nothing. Baby steps. They could do baby steps.

But one thing was nonnegotiable. "You have to apologize to him."

"Daughter, I hardly think that's necessary."

Of course she wouldn't. Apologizing meant acknowledging she was wrong. But if Elle backed down now, she'd run the risk of her mom trying to steamroll her at every opportunity. This entire conversation would have been for nothing. "You wouldn't have let me get away with being rude to a guest, and Gabe's going to be family."

"You haven't said yes yet." At her glare, her mother sighed again. "Fine, I'll apologize."

Elle stood. "Let's get on that, then." If they waited too long, Gabe might reconsider that whole forever thing and take off. When they walked back into the dining room, though, he was exactly where she'd left him. Elle cleared her throat.

Her mom smoothed down her skirt again. "It's been brought to my attention that I've been unforgivably rude. I'm terribly sorry." Her tone said otherwise, but this was as good as they were going to get. She'd warm up to Gabe as time went on. Or maybe she wouldn't. It didn't really matter, because he was looking at Elle with such pride and love that her chest got tight. She rounded the table and sank into the chair next to him, immediately taking his hand again.

The rest of dinner wasn't the most comfortable, but at least her mom managed to make it through without any more snide comments. Still, Elle didn't draw a full breath until she and Gabe were back in his car and speeding through the darkness. "Oh my God, I can't believe it." Every bone in her body disappeared and she slumped into the seat, shaking. "I browbeat my mom into apologizing."

Gabe slowed and pulled off the road. "Are you okay?"

"Yeah, just…give me a minute." She waved her hand, wondering that it wasn't shaking. "That was absolutely terrible."

"I was just going to say that I thought it'd gone well."

"You're crazy." But she smiled. "You really want to marry me?"

"Babe, of course I want to marry you. After I got your father's permission, I was planning on proposing in a few weeks when we went to pick pumpkins up at Greenbluff. It wasn't supposed to come out like this." He ran his hand over his face. "I, ah, lost my temper in there."

She sat up. "I love you."

"You aren't disappointed? I can still whip out a decent proposal."

"You're the only thing that matters." Not six months ago, she would have been disappointed that the proposal wasn't everything she'd always dreamed. Then again, six months ago she hadn't met Gabe and discovered how perfect non-perfect relationships were. None of it mattered but the fact they were together.

Gabe reached across the seat and opened the

glove box. He pulled out a distinctive square box. "Then, Elle Walser, would you do me the honor of being my wife?"

She didn't even give him a chance to open the box. "Yes, yes, so much yes." Elle kissed him, trying to put all her love and the crazy spiral of beyond-happy emotions she was experiencing into it. And then his tongue stroked hers, and everything washed away but the sheer joy of knowing this man was hers. Forever.

Headlights cut across the windshield and Gabe pulled back. "If we don't stop now, someone's going to end up with an eyeful." He kissed her again. "And you need to look at the ring."

Oh, right. The ring. Elle bit her lip as he opened the box. The design was deceptively simple—a princess-cut diamond, nestled in the middle of six smaller stones on a white-gold band—but there was no mistaking the quality. That rock was freaking huge. "That is... Holy crap, Gabe."

"Do you hate it? We can get something different."

Tears pricked her eyes and it was suddenly really difficult to swallow. "I don't hate it." Elle sniffed a little as Gabe slipped the giant diamond onto her finger. It fit perfectly. "I love it. I love you."

"I love you too, babe. Let's get home and try out that spin cycle."

She laughed, just like he'd obviously wanted her to, and settled back into her seat. It was only once they were moving again that Elle said, "Now all we need to do is break the news to my brother."

Did you love Gabe and Elle's story?

Be sure to check out

CHASING MRS. RIGHT

the next book in the Come Undone series
by Katee Robert

Coming Spring 2013

ACKNOWLEDGMENTS

To God, for the epically awesome timing and inspiration for this piece.

To Heather Howland, for being Ultimate Brainstorming Champion. I really look forward to conquering more "bad" tropes with you!

To Seleste Delaney, for answering questions most people would be calling the cops on me for and for always being there to calm my panicked "OMG THIS HAPPENED" freak-outs.

To Candace Havens, for hosting the Fast Draft course. This book couldn't have been put together in time if not for that accountability.

And to my mom, for never giving me the evil eye for showing up unannounced for dinner with two kids in tow, and for being just as geeked out over my books as I am. I love you!

Now in paperback...

SEDUCING CINDERELLA
the first book in the Fighting for Love series by

New York Times Bestselling Author
Gina L. Maxwell

He'll teach her the art of seduction...for a price.

Mixed martial arts fighter Reid Andrews's chance to reclaim his title as light heavyweight champ is shattered when he's injured only months before the rematch. To make sure he's healed in time, his trainer sends him to recuperate under a professional's care—Reid's best friend's little sister, all grown up.

Disorganized and bookish Lucie Miller needs some professional help of her own. She'd do anything to catch the eye of a doctor she's crushed on for years, so when Reid offers seduction lessons in exchange for 24/7 conditioning for the biggest fight of his career, Lucie jumps at the chance.

Soon Reid finds himself in the fight of his life...winning Lucie's heart before she gives it to someone else.

Unleash your inner vixen with these sexy bestselling Brazen releases...

Private Practice by **Samanthe Beck**

Dr. Ellie Swan is determined to win the heart of her town's golden boy. There's only one problem—he wants a skilled, sexually adventurous partner. Armed with *The Wild Woman's Guide to Sex* and lessons from sex-on-a-stick bad boy Tyler Longfoot, Ellie is confident she can become what he needs....if she doesn't fall for Tyler first.

Recipe for Satisfaction by **Gina Gordon**

Famous bad boy restaurateur Jack Vaughn is trying to find his way back to the living when he meets the beautiful Sterling Andrews, the professional organizer hell-bent on seducing the tattooed hottie as part of her fresh take on life. Too bad she's Jack's newest employee, and totally off-limits.

Protecting What's His by **Tessa Bailey**

Ginger Peet just committed the perfect crime to save her sister from their abusive home. But the girls' new neighbor, straight-laced homicide lieutenant Derek Tyler, knows something's up. He won't rest until Ginger's his—completely—but can Derek protect her from the danger she's unwittingly stumbled into?

Vanilla on Top by C.J. Ellisson

Determined to leave her wallflower tendencies at the door, Heather Pierce attends a speed dating event pretending to be someone new. Someone *dominant*. Little does she know, the man whose world she rocks isn't about to let the mysterious vixen slip through his grasp.

Her Forbidden Hero by Laura Kaye

Former Army Special Forces Sgt. Marco Vieri has never thought of Alyssa Scott as more than his best friend's little sister, but her return home changes that. Now that she's back in his life, will he become her forbidden hero, and can she heal him, one touch at a time?

One Night with a Hero by Laura Kaye

After growing up with an abusive, alcoholic father, Army Special Forces Sgt. Brady Scott vowed never to have a family of his own. But when a hot one-night stand with new neighbor Joss Daniels leads to an unexpected pregnancy, can he let go of his past and create a new future with her?

Tempting the Best Man by J. Lynn

Madison Daniels has worshipped her brother's best friend since they were kids, but they've blurred the lines before and now they can't stop bickering. Forced together for her brother's wedding getaway, will they call a truce or strangle each other first?

Tempting the Player by J. Lynn

After the paparazzi catches him in a compromising position, baseball bad boy Chad Gamble is issued an ultimatum: fake falling in love with the feisty redhead in the pictures, or kiss his multi-million dollar contract goodbye. Too bad being blackmailed into a relationship with Chad is the last thing Bridget Rodgers needs.

Down for the Count by **Christine Bell**

After Lacey Garrity's wedding day goes horribly, adulterously wrong, she shucks her straight-laced life and accepts a reckless challenge from sexy boxer Galen Thomas, her best friend's older brother. The dare? Take him on her honeymoon instead, but will running away with the enemy lead Lacey to love?

No Flowers Required by **Cari Quinn**

A night of passion is all down-on-her-luck flower shop owner Alexa Conroy wants, but when she propositions a sexy stranger, she gets more than she bargained for. Dillon James isn't who he says he is. Will saving her company be enough to protect their love from Dillon's lies?